William Edward Simonds

De Quincey's Revolt of the Tartars

William Edward Simonds

De Quincey's Revolt of the Tartars

1st Edition | ISBN: 978-3-75236-346-3

Place of Publication: Frankfurt am Main, Germany

Year of Publication: 2020

Outlook Verlag GmbH, Germany.

DE QUINCEY'S

REVOLT OF THE TARTARS

BY

WILLIAM EDWARD SIMONDS

PREFACE.

In editing an English classic for use in the secondary schools, there is always opportunity for the expression of personal convictions and personal taste; nevertheless, where one has predecessors in the task of preparing such a text, it is difficult always, occasionally impossible, to avoid treading on their heels. The present editor, therefore, hastens to acknowledge his indebtedness to the various school editions of the *Revolt of the Tartars*, already in existence. The notes by Masson are so authoritative and so essential that their quotation needs no comment. De Quincey's footnotes are retained in their original form and appear embodied in the text. The other annotations suggest the method which the editor would follow in class-room work upon this essay.

The student's attention is called frequently to the *form* of expression; the discriminating use of epithets, the employment of foreign phrases, the allusions to Milton and the Bible, the structure of paragraphs, the treatment of incident, the development of feeling, the impressiveness of a present personality; all this, however, is with the purpose, not of mechanic exercise, nor merely to illustrate "rhetoric," but to illuminate *De Quincey*. It is with this intention, presumably, that the text is prescribed. There is little attractiveness, after all, in the idea of a style so colorless and so impersonal that the individuality of its victim is lost in its own perfection; this was certainly not the Opium-Eater's mind concerning literary form, nor does it appear to have been the aim of any of our masters. Indeed, it may be well in passing to point out to pupils how fatal to success in writing is the attempt to imitate the style of any man, De Quincey included; it is always in order to emphasize the naturalness and spontaneity of the "grand style" wherever it is found. The teacher should not inculcate a blind admiration of all that De Quincey has said or done; there is opportunity, even in this brief essay, to exercise the pupil in applying the commonplace tests of criticism, although it should be seen to as well that a true appreciation is awakened for the real excellences of this little masterpiece.

INTRODUCTION.

Thomas De Quincey is one of the eccentric figures in English literature. Popularly he is known as the English Opium-Eater and as the subject of numerous anecdotes which emphasize the oddities of his temperament and the unconventionality of his habits. That this man of distinguished genius was the victim—pitifully the victim—of opium is the lamentable fact; that he was morbidly shy and shunned intercourse with all except a few intimate, congenial friends; that he was comically indifferent to the fashion of his dress; that he was the most unpractical and childlike of men; that he was often betrayed, because of these peculiarities, into many ridiculous embarrassments, such as are described by Mr. Findlay, Mr. Hogg, and Mr. Burton,—of all this there can be no doubt; but these idiosyncrasies are, after all, of minor importance, the accidents, not the essentials in the life and personality of this remarkable man. The points that should attract our notice, the qualities that really give distinction to De Quincey, are the broad sweep of his knowledge, almost unlimited in its scope and singularly accurate in its details, a facility of phrasing and a word supply that transformed the mere power of discriminating expression into a fine art, and a style that, while it lapsed occasionally from the standard of its own excellence, was generally self-corrective and frequently forsook the levels of commonplace excellence for the highest reaches of impassioned prose. Nor is this all. His pages do not lack in humor—humor of the truest and most delicate type; and if De Quincey is at times impelled beyond the bounds of taste, even these excursions demonstrate his power, at least in handling the grotesque. His sympathies, however, are always genuine, and often are profound. The pages of his autobiographic essays reveal the strength of his affections, while in the interpretation of such a character as that of Joan of Arc, or in allusions like those to the pariahs,—defenceless outcasts from society, by whose wretched lot his heart was often wrung,—he writes in truest pathos.

Now sympathy is own child of the imagination, whether expressed in the language of laughter or in the vernacular of tears; and the most distinctive quality in the mental make-up of De Quincey was, after all, this dominant imagination which was characteristic of the man from childhood to old age. The Opium-Eater once defined the *great scholar* as "not one who depends simply on an infinite memory, but also on an infinite and electrical power of combination, bringing together from the four winds, like the angel of the resurrection, what else were dust from dead men's bones, into the unity of breathing life." Such was De Quincey himself. He was a scholar born, gifted with a mind apt for the subtleties of metaphysics, a memory well-nigh

3

inexhaustible in the recovery of facts; in one respect, at least, he was a *great* scholar, for his mind was dominated by an imagination as vigorous as that which created Macaulay's *England*, almost as sensitive to dramatic effect as that which painted Carlyle's *French Revolution*. Therefore when he wrote narrative, historical narrative, or reminiscence, he lived in the experiences he pictured, as great historians do; perhaps living over again the scenes of the past, or for the first time making real the details of occurrences with which he was only recently familiar.

The *Revolt of the Tartars* is a good illustration of his power. Attracted by the chance reading of an obscure French missionary and traveller to the dramatic possibilities of an episode in Russian history, De Quincey built from the bare notes thus discovered, supplemented by others drawn from a matter-of-fact German archæologist, a narrative which for vividness of detail and truthfulness of local color belongs among the best of those classics in which fancy helps to illuminate fact, and where the imagination is invoked to recreate what one feels intuitively must have been real.

The *Revolt of the Tartars*, while not exhibiting the highest achievement of the author's power, nevertheless belongs in the group of writings wherein his peculiar excellences are fairly manifested. The obvious quality of its realism has been pointed out already; the masterly use of the principles of suspense and stimulated interest will hardly pass unnoticed. A negative excellence is the absence of that discursiveness in composition, that tendency to digress into superfluous comment, which is this author's one prevailing fault. De Quincey was gifted with a fine appreciation of harmonious sound, and in those passages where his spirit soars highest not the least of their beauties is found in the melodiousness of their tone and the rhythmic sweetness of their motion.

It is as a master of rhetoric that De Quincey is distinguished among writers. Some hints of his ability are seen in the opening and closing passages of this essay, but to find him at his best one must turn to the *Confessions* and to the other papers which describe his life, particularly those which recount his marvellous dreams. In these papers we find the passages where De Quincey's passion rises to the heights which few other writers have ever reached in prose, a loftiness and grandeur which is technically denominated as "sublime." In his *Essay on Style*, published in *Blackwood's*, 1840, he deprecates the usual indifference to form, on the part of English writers, "the tendency of the national mind to value the matter of a book not only as paramount to the manner, but even as distinct from it and as capable of a separate insulation." As one of the great masters of prose style in this century, De Quincey has so served the interests of art in this regard, that in his own case the charge is sometimes reversed: his own works are read rather to observe his manner than to absorb his thought. Yet when this is said, it is not to imply that the material is unworthy or the ideas unsound; on the contrary, his sentiment is true and his ideas are wholesome; but many of the topics treated lie outside the deeper interests of ordinary life, and fail to appeal to us so practically as do the writings of some lesser men. Of the "one hundred and fifty magazine articles" which comprise his works, there are many that will not claim the general interest, yet his writings as a whole will always be recognized by students of rhetoric as containing excellences which place their author among the English classics. Nor can De Quincey be accused of subordinating matter to manner; in spite of his taste for the theatrical and a tendency to extravagance, his expression is in keeping with his thought, and the material of those passages which contain his most splendid flights is appropriate to the treatment it receives. One effective reason, certainly, why we take pleasure in the mere style of De Quincey's work is because that work is so thoroughly inspired with the Opium-Eater's own genial personality, because it so unmistakably suggests that inevitable "smack of individuality" which gives to the productions of all great authors their truest distinction if not their greatest worth.

Thomas De Quincey was born in Manchester, August 15, 1785. His father was a well-to-do merchant of literary taste, but of him the children of the household scarcely knew; he was an invalid, a prey to consumption, and during their childhood made his residence mostly in the milder climate of Lisbon or the West Indies. Thomas was seven years old when his father was brought home to die, and the lad, though sensitively impressed by the event, felt little of the significance of relationship between them. Mrs. De Quincey was a somewhat stately lady, rather strict in discipline and rigid in her views. There does not seem to have been the most complete sympathy between mother and son, yet De Quincey was always reverent in his attitude, and certainly entertained a genuine respect for her intelligence and character. There were eight children in the home, four sons and four daughters; Thomas was the fifth in age, and his relations to the other members of this little community are set forth most interestingly in the opening chapters of his *Autobiographic Sketches.*

De Quincey's child life was spent in the country; first at a pretty rustic dwelling known as "The Farm," and after 1792 at a larger country house near Manchester, built by his father, and given by his mother the pleasantly suggestive name of "Greenhay," *hay* meaning hedge, or hedgerow. The early boyhood of Thomas De Quincey is of more than ordinary interest, because of the clear light it throws upon the peculiar temperament and endowments of the man. Moreover, we have the best of authority in our study of this period, namely, the author himself, who in the *Sketches* already mentioned, and in his most noted work, *The Confessions of an English Opium-Eater*, has told the story of these early years in considerable detail and with apparent sincerity. De Quincey was not a sturdy boy. Shy and dreamy, exquisitely sensitive to impressions of melancholy and mystery, he was endowed with an imagination abnormally active even for a child. It is customary to give prominence to De Quincey's pernicious habit of opium-eating, in attempting to explain the grotesque fancies and weird flights of his marvellous mind in later years; yet it is only fair to emphasize the fact that the later achievements of that strange creative faculty were clearly foreshadowed in youth. For example, the earliest incident in his life that he could afterwards recall, he describes as "a remarkable dream of terrific grandeur about a favorite nurse, which is interesting to myself for this reason—that it demonstrates my dreaming tendencies to have been constitutional, and not dependent upon laudanum." [1] Again he tells us how, when six years old, upon the death of a favorite sister three years older, he stole unobserved upstairs to the death chamber; unlocking the door and entering silently, he stood for a moment gazing through the open window toward the bright sunlight of a cloudless day, then turned to behold the angel face upon the pillow. Awed in the presence of death, the meaning of which he began vaguely to understand, he stood listening to a "solemn wind" that began to blow—"the saddest that ear ever heard." What followed should appear in De Quincey's own words: "A vault seemed to open in the zenith of the far blue sky, a shaft which ran up forever. I, in spirit, rose as if on billows that also ran up the shaft forever; and the billows seemed to pursue the throne of God; but *that* also ran on before us and fled away continually. The flight and the pursuit seemed to go on forever and ever. Frost gathering frost, some sarsar wind of death, seemed to repel me; some mighty relation between God and death dimly struggled to evolve itself from the dreadful antagonism between them; shadowy meanings even yet continued to exercise and torment, in dreams, the deciphering oracle within me. I slept—for how long I cannot say: slowly I recovered my self-possession; and, when I woke, found myself standing as before, close to my sister's bed." [2] Somewhat similar in effect were the fancies that came to this dreamy boy on Sunday mornings during service in the fine old English church. Through the wide central field of uncolored glass, set in a rich framework of gorgeous color,—for the side panes of the great windows were pictured with the stories of saints and martyrs,—the lad saw "white fleecy clouds sailing over the azure depths of the sky." Straightway the picture changed in his imagination, and visions of young children, lying on white beds of sickness and of death, rose before his eyes, ascending slowly and softly into heaven, God's arms descending from the heavens that He might the sooner take them to Himself and grant release. Such are not infrequently the

6

dreams of children. De Quincey's experience is not unique; but with him imagination, the imagination of childhood, remained unimpaired through life. It was not wholly opium that made him the great dreamer of our literature, any more than it was the effect of a drug that brought from his dying lips the cry of "Sister, sister, sister!"—an echo from this sacred chamber of death, where he had stood awed and entranced nearly seventy years before.

Not all of De Quincey's boyhood, however, was passed under influences so serious and mystical as these. He was early compelled to undergo what he is pleased to call his "introduction to the world of strife." His brother William, five years the senior of Thomas, appears to have been endowed with an imagination as remarkable as his own. "His genius for mischief," says Thomas, "amounted to inspiration." Very amusing are the chronicles of the little autocracy thus despotized by William. The assumption of the young tyrant was magnificent. Along with the prerogatives and privileges of seniority, he took upon himself as well certain responsibilities more galling to his half-dozen uneasy subordinates, doubtless, than the undisputed hereditary rights of age. William constituted himself the educational guide of the nursery, proclaiming theories, delivering lectures, performing experiments, asserting opinions upon subjects diverse and erudite. Indeed, a vigorous spirit was housed in William's body, and but for his early death, this lad also might have brought lustre to the family name.

A real introduction to the world of strife came with the development of a lively feud between the two brothers on the one side, and on the other a crowd of young belligerents employed in a cotton factory on the road between Greenhay and Manchester, where the boys now attended school. Active hostilities occurred daily when the two "aristocrats" passed the factory on their way home at the hour when its inmates emerged from their labor. The dread of this encounter hung like a cloud over Thomas, yet he followed William loyally, and served with all the spirit of a cadet of the house. Imagination played an important part in this campaign, and it is for that reason primarily that to this and the other incidents of De Quincey's childhood prominence is here given; in no better way can we come to an understanding of the real nature of this singular man.

In 1796 the home at Greenhay was broken up. The irrepressible William was sent to London to study art; Mrs. De Quincey removed to Bath, and Thomas was placed in the grammar school of that town; a younger brother, Richard, in all respects a pleasing contrast to William, was a sympathetic comrade and schoolmate. For two years De Quincey remained in this school, achieving a great reputation in the study of Latin, and living a congenial, comfortable life. This was followed by a year in a private school at Winkfield, which was terminated by an invitation to travel in Ireland with young Lord Westport, a lad of De Quincey's own age, an intimacy having sprung up between them a year earlier at Bath. It was in 1800 that the trip was made, and the period of the visit extended over four or five months. After this long recess De Quincey was placed in the grammar school at Manchester, his guardians expecting that a three years' course in this school would bring him a scholarship at Oxford. However, the new environment proved wholly uncongenial, and the sensitive boy who, in spite of his shyness and his slender frame, possessed grit in abundance, and who was through life more or less a law to himself, made up his mind to run away. His flight was significant. Early on a July morning he slipped quietly off—in one pocket a copy of an English poet, a volume of Euripides in the other. His first move was toward Chester, the seventeen-year-old runaway deeming it proper that he should report at once to his mother, who was now living in that town. So he trudged overland forty miles and faced his astonished and indignant parent. At the suggestion of a kind-hearted uncle, just home from India, Thomas was let off easily; indeed, he was given an allowance of a guinea a week, with permission to go on a tramp through North Wales, a proposition which he hailed with delight. The next three months were spent in a rather pleasant ramble, although the weekly allowance was scarcely sufficient to supply all the comforts desired. The trip ended strangely. Some sudden fancy seizing him, the boy broke off all connection with his friends and went to London. Unknown, unprovided for, he buried himself in the vast life of the metropolis. He lived a precarious existence for several months, suffering from exposure, reduced to the verge of starvation, his whereabouts a mystery to his friends. The cloud of this experience hung darkly over his spirit, even in later manhood; perceptions of a true world of strife were vivid; impressions of these wretched months formed the material of his most sombre dreams.

Rescued at last, providentially, De Quincey spent the next period of his life, covering the years 1803-7, in residence at Oxford. His career as a student at the university is obscure. He was a member of Worcester College, was known as a quiet, studious man, and lived an isolated if not a solitary life. With a German student, who taught him Hebrew, De Quincey seems to have had some intimacy, but his circle of acquaintance was small, and no contemporary has thrown much light on his stay. In 1807 he disappeared from Oxford, having taken the written tests for his degree, but failing to present himself for the necessary oral examination.

The year of his departure from Oxford brought to De Quincey a long-coveted pleasure—acquaintance with two famous contemporaries whom he greatly admired, Coleridge and Wordsworth. Characteristic of De Quincey in many ways was his gift, anonymously made, of £300 to his hero, Coleridge. This was in 1807, when De Quincey was twenty-two, and was master of his inheritance. The acquaintance ripened into intimacy, and in 1809 the young man, himself gifted with talents which were to make him equally famous with these, took up his residence at Grasmere, in the Lake country, occupying for many years the cottage which Wordsworth had given up on his removal to ampler quarters at Rydal Mount. Here he spent much of his time in the society of the men who were then grouped in distinguished neighborhood; besides Wordsworth and Coleridge, the poet Southey was accessible, and a frequent visitor was John Wilson, later widely known as the "Christopher North" of *Blackwood's Magazine*. Nor was De Quincey idle; his habits of study were confirmed; indeed, he was already a philosopher at twenty-four. These were years of hard reading and industrious thought, wherein he accumulated much of that metaphysical wisdom which was afterward to win admiring recognition.

In 1816 De Quincey married Margaret Simpson, a farmer's daughter living near. There is a pretty scene painted by the author himself, [3] in which he gives us a glimpse of his domestic life at this time. Therein he pictures the cottage, standing in a valley, eighteen miles from any town; no spacious valley, but about two miles long by three-quarters of a mile in average width. The mountains are real mountains, between 3000 and 4000 feet high, and the cottage a real cottage, white, embowered with flowering shrubs, so chosen as to unfold a succession of flowers upon the walls, and clustering around the windows, through all the months of spring, summer, and autumn, beginning, in fact, with May roses and ending with jasmine. It is in the winter season, however, that De Quincey paints his picture, and so he describes a room, seventeen feet by twelve, and not more than seven and one-half feet high. This is the drawing-room, although it might more justly be termed the library, for it happens that books are the one form of property in which the owner is wealthy. Of these he has about 5000, collected gradually since his eighteenth year. The room is, therefore, populous with books. There is a good fire on the hearth. The furniture is plain and modest, befitting the unpretending cottage of a scholar. Near the fire stands a tea table; there are only two cups and saucers on the tray. It is an "eternal" teapot that the artist would like us to imagine, for he usually drinks tea from eight o'clock at night to four in the morning. There is, of course, a companion at the tea table, and very lovingly does the husband suggest the pleasant personality of his young wife. One other important feature is included in the scene; upon the table there rests also a decanter, in which sparkles the ruby-colored laudanum.

De Quincey's experience with opium had begun while he was a student at the university, in 1804. It was first taken to obtain relief from neuralgia, and his use of the drug did not at once become habitual. During the period of residence at Grasmere, however, De Quincey became confirmed in the habit, and so thoroughly was he its victim that for a season his intellectual powers were well-nigh paralyzed; his mind sank under such a cloud of depression and gloom that his condition was pitiful in the extreme. Just before his marriage, in 1816, De Quincey, by a vigorous effort, partially regained his self-control and succeeded in materially reducing his daily allowance of the drug; but in the following year he fell more deeply than ever under its baneful power, until in 1818-19 his consumption of opium was something almost incredible. Thus he became truly enough the great English Opium-Eater, whose Confessions were later to fill a unique place in English literature. It was finally the absolute need of bettering his financial condition that compelled De Quincey to shake off the shackles of his vice; this he practically accomplished, although perhaps he was never entirely free from the habit. The event is coincident with the beginning of his career as a public writer. In 1820 he became a man of letters.

As a professional writer it is to be noted that De Quincey was throughout a contributor to the periodicals. With one or two exceptions all his works found their way to the public through the pages of the magazines, and he was associated as contributor with most of those that were prominent in his time. From 1821 to 1825 we find him residing for the most part in London, and here his public career began. It was De Quincey's most distinctive work which first appeared. The *London Magazine*, in its issue for September, 1821, contained the first paper of the *Confessions of an English Opium-Eater*. The novelty of the subject was sufficient to obtain for the new writer an interested hearing, and there was much discussion as to whether his apparent frankness was genuine or assumed. All united in applause of the masterly style which distinguished the essay, also of the profundity and value of the interesting material it contained. A second part was included in the magazine for October. Other articles by the Opium-Eater followed, in which the wide scholarship of the author was abundantly shown, although the topics were of less general interest.

In 1826 De Quincey became an occasional contributor to *Blackwood's Magazine*, and this connection drew him to Edinburgh, where he remained, either in the city itself or in its vicinity, for the rest of his life. The grotesquely humorous *Essay on Murder Considered as One of the Fine Arts* appeared in *Blackwood's* in 1827. In 1832 he published a series of articles on Roman History, entitled *The Cæsars*. It was in July, 1837, that the *Revolt of the Tartars* appeared; in 1840 his critical paper upon *The Essenes*. Meanwhile De Quincey had begun contributions to *Tait's Magazine*, another Edinburgh publication, and it was in that periodical that the *Sketches of Life and Manners from the Autobiography of an English Opium-Eater* began to appear in 1834, running on through several years. These sketches include the chapters on Wordsworth, Coleridge, Lamb, and Southey as well as those *Autobiographic Sketches* which form such a charming and illuminating portion of his complete works.

The family life was sadly broken in 1837 by the death of De Quincey's wife. He who was now left as guardian of the little household of six children, was himself so helpless in all practical matters that it seemed as though he were in their childish care rather than protector of them. Scores of anecdotes are related of his odd and unpractical behavior. One of his curious habits had been the multiplication of lodgings; as books and manuscripts accumulated about him so that there remained room for no more, he would turn the key upon his possessions and migrate elsewhere to repeat the performance later on. It is known that as many as four separate rents were at one and the same time being paid by this odd, shy little man, rather than allow the disturbance or contraction of his domain. Sometimes an anxious journey in search of a manuscript had to be made by author and publisher in conjunction before the missing paper could be located. The home life of this eccentric yet lovable man of genius seems to have been always affectionate and tender in spite even of his bondage to opium; it was especially beautiful and childlike in his latest years. His eldest daughter, Margaret, assumed quietly the place of headship, and with a discretion equal to her devotion she watched over her father's welfare. With reference to De Quincey's circumstances at this time, his biographer, Mr. Masson, says: "Very soon, if left to himself, he would have taken possession of every room in the house, one after another, and 'snowed up' each with his papers; but, that having been gently prevented, he had one room to work in all day and all night to his heart's content. The evenings, or the intervals between his daily working time and his nightly working time, or stroll, he generally spent in the drawing-room with his daughters, either alone or in company with any friends that chanced to be with him. At such times, we are told, he was unusually charming. 'The newspaper was brought out, and he, telling in his own delightful way, rather than reading, the news, would, on questions from this one or that one of the party, often including young friends of his children, neighbors, or visitors from distant places, illuminate the subject with such a wealth of memories, of old stories of past or present experiences, of humor, of suggestion, even of prophecy, as by its very wealth makes it impossible to give any taste of it.' The description is by one of his daughters; and she adds a touch which is inimitable in its fidelity and tenderness. 'He was not,' she says, 'a reassuring man for nervous people to live with, as those nights were exceptional on which he did not set something on fire, the commonest incident being for some one to look up from book or work, to say casually, *Papa, your hair is on fire*; of which a calm *Is it, my love?* and a hand rubbing out the blaze was all the notice taken.'" [4]

Of his personal appearance Professor Minto says:

"He was a slender little man, with small, clearly chiselled features, a large head, and a remarkably high, square forehead. There was a peculiarly high and regular arch in the wrinkles of his brow, which was also slightly contracted. The lines of his countenance fell naturally into an expression of mild suffering, of endurance sweetened by benevolence, or, according to the fancy of the interpreter, of gentle, melancholy sweetness. All that met him seem to have been struck with the measured, silvery, yet somewhat hollow and unearthly tones of his voice, the more impressive that the flow of his talk was unhesitating and unbroken."

The literary labors were continuous. In 1845 the beautiful *Suspiria de Profundis* (Sighs from the Depths) appeared in *Blackwood's*; *The English Mail Coach* and *The Vision of Sudden Death*, in 1849. Among other papers contributed to *Tait's Magazine*, the *Joan of Arc* appeared in 1847. During the last ten years of his life, De Quincey was occupied chiefly in preparing for the publishers a complete edition of his works. Ticknor & Fields, of Boston, the most distinguished of our American publishing firms, had put forth, 1851-55, the first edition of De Quincey's collected writings, in twenty volumes. The first British edition was undertaken by Mr. James Hogg, of Edinburgh, in 1853, with the co-operation of the author, and under his direction; the final volume of this edition was not issued until the year following De Quincey's death.

In the autumn of 1859 the frail physique of the now famous Opium-Eater grew gradually feeble, although suffering from no definite disease. It became evident that his life was drawing to its end. On December 8, his two daughters standing by his side, he fell into a doze. His mind had been wandering amid the scenes of his childhood, and his last utterance was the cry, "Sister, sister, sister!" as if in recognition of one awaiting him, one who had been often in his dreams, the beloved Elizabeth, whose death had made so profound and lasting an impression on his imagination as a child.

The authoritative edition of *De Quincey's Works* is that edited by David Masson and published in fourteen volumes by Adam and Charles Black (Edinburgh). For American students the *Riverside Edition*, in twelve volumes (Houghton, Mifflin & Co., Boston), will be found convenient. The most satisfactory *Life of De Quincey* is the one by Masson in the *English Men of*

12

Letters series. Of a more anecdotal type are the *Life of De Quincey*, by H.A. Page, whose real name is Alexander H. Japp (2 vols., New York, 1877), and *De Quincey Memorials* (New York, 1891), by the same author. Very interesting is the brief volume, *Recollections of Thomas De Quincey*, by John R. Findlay (Edinburgh, 1886), who also contributes the paper on *De Quincey* to the *Encyclopædia Britannica*. *De Quincey and his Friends*, by James Hogg (London, 1895), is another volume of recollections, souvenirs, and anecdotes, which help to make real their subject's personality. Besides the editor, other writers contribute to this volume: Richard Woodhouse, John R. Findlay, and John Hill Burton, who has given under the name "Papaverius," a picturesque description of the Opium-Eater. The student should always remember that De Quincey's own chapters in the *Autobiographic Sketches*, and the *Confessions of an English Opium-Eater*, which are among the most charming and important of his writings, are also the most authoritative and most valuable sources of our information concerning him. In reading about De Quincey, do not fail to read De Quincey himself.

The best criticism of the Opium-Eater's work is found in William Minto's *Manual of English Prose Literature* (Ginn & Co.). A shorter essay is contained in Saintsbury's *History of Nineteenth Century Literature*. A very valuable list of all De Quincey's writings, in chronological order, is given by Fred N. Scott, in his edition of De Quincey's essays on *Style, Rhetoric*, and *Language* (Allyn & Bacon). Numerous magazine articles may be found by referring to Poole's Index.

FOOTNOTES:

[1] *Autobiographic Sketches*, Chap. I.

[2] *Ibid.*

[3] *Confessions of an English Opium-Eater*, Part II.

[4] *De Quincey (English Men of Letters)*, David Masson, p. 110.

HOW TO READ DE QUINCEY.

"De Quincey's sixteen volumes of magazine articles are full of brain from beginning to end. At the rate of about half a volume a day, they would serve for a month's reading, and a month continuously might be worse expended. There are few courses of reading from which a young man of good natural intelligence would come away more instructed, charmed, and stimulated, or, to express the matter as definitely as possible, with his mind more *stretched*. Good natural intelligence, a certain fineness of fibre, and some amount of scholarly education, have to be presupposed, indeed, in all readers of De Quincey. But, even for the fittest readers, a month's complete and continuous course of De Quincey would be too much. Better have him on the shelf, and take down a volume at intervals for one or two of the articles to which there may be an immediate attraction. An evening with De Quincey in this manner will always be profitable."

DAVID MASSON, Life of De Quincey, Chap. XI.

REVOLT OF THE TARTARS;

OR, FLIGHT OF THE KALMUCK KHAN AND HIS PEOPLE
FROM THE RUSSIAN TERRITORIES TO THE
FRONTIERS OF CHINA.

There is no great event in modern history, or, perhaps it may be said more broadly, none in all history, from its earliest records, less generally known, or more striking to the imagination, than the flight eastwards of a principal Tartar nation across the boundless steppes of Asia in the 5 latter half of the last century. The *terminus a quo* of this flight and the *terminus ad quem* are equally magnificent—the mightiest of Christian thrones being the one, the mightiest of pagan the other; and the grandeur of these two terminal objects is harmoniously supported by the 10 romantic circumstances of the flight. In the abruptness of its commencement and the fierce velocity of its execution we read an expression of the wild, barbaric character of the agents. In the unity of purpose connecting this myriad of wills, and in the blind but unerring aim at a 15 mark so remote, there is something which recalls to the mind those almighty instincts that propel the migrations of the swallow and the leeming or the life-withering marches of the locust. Then, again, in the gloomy vengeance of Russia and her vast artillery, which hung upon the rear 20 and the skirts of the fugitive vassals, we are reminded of Miltonic images—such, for instance, as that of the solitary hand pursuing through desert spaces and through ancient chaos a rebellious host, and overtaking with volleying thunders those who believed themselves already within the security of darkness and of distance.

I shall have occasion, farther on, to compare this event with other great national catastrophes as to the magnitude 5 of the suffering. But it may also challenge a comparison with similar events under another relation,—viz. as to its dramatic capabilities. Few cases, perhaps, in romance or history, can sustain a close collation with this as to the *complexity* of its separate interests. The great outline of 10 the enterprise, taken in connection with the operative motives, hidden or avowed, and the religious sanctions under which it was pursued, give to the case a triple character: 1st, That of a *conspiracy*, with as close a unity in the incidents, and as much of a personal interest in 15 the moving characters, with fine dramatic contrasts, as belongs to "Venice Preserved" or to the "Fiesco" of Schiller. 2dly, That of a great military expedition offering

the same romantic features of vast distances to be
traversed, vast reverses to be sustained, untried routes, 20
enemies obscurely ascertained, and hardships too vaguely
prefigured, which mark the Egyptian expedition of Cambyses—
the
anabasis of the younger Cyrus, and the
subsequent retreat of the ten thousand, the Parthian
expeditions of the Romans, especially those of Crassus 25
and Julian—or (as more disastrous than any of them,
and, in point of space, as well as in amount of forces,
more extensive) the Russian anabasis and katabasis of
Napoleon. 3dly, That of a religious *Exodus*, authorized
by an oracle venerated throughout many nations of Asia, 30
—an Exodus, therefore, in so far resembling the great
Scriptural Exodus of the Israelites, under Moses and
Joshua, as well as in the very peculiar distinction of carrying
along with them their entire families, women, children,
slaves, their herd of cattle and of sheep, their horses and
their camels.

   This triple character of the enterprise naturally invests
it with a more comprehensive interest; but the dramatic
interest which we ascribed to it, or its fitness for a stage 5
representation, depends partly upon the marked variety
and the strength of the personal agencies concerned, and
partly upon the succession of scenical situations. Even
the steppes, the camels, the tents, the snowy and the sandy
deserts are not beyond the scale of our modern representative 10
powers, as often called into action in the theatres
both of Paris and London; and the series of situations
unfolded,—beginning with the general conflagration on
the Wolga—passing thence to the disastrous scenes of
the flight (as it *literally* was in its commencement)—to 15
the Tartar siege of the Russian fortress Koulagina—the
bloody engagement with the Cossacks in the mountain
passes at Ouchim—the surprisal by the Bashkirs and
the advanced posts of the Russian army at Torgau—the
private conspiracy at this point against the Khan—the 20
long succession of running fights—the parting massacres
at the Lake of Tengis under the eyes of the Chinese—and,
finally, the tragical retribution to Zebek-Dorchi at
the hunting lodge of the Chinese Emperor;—all these

situations communicate a *scenical* animation to the wild 25
romance, if treated dramatically; whilst a higher and a
philosophic interest belongs to it as a case of authentic
history, commemorating a great revolution, for good and
for evil, in the fortunes of a whole people—a people semi-
barbarous,
but simple-hearted, and of ancient descent. 30

   On the 21st of January, 1761, the young Prince Oubacha
assumed the sceptre of the Kalmucks upon the death
of his father. Some part of the power attached to this
dignity he had already wielded since his fourteenth year,
in quality of Vice-Khan, by the express appointment and
with the avowed support of the Russian Government.
He was now about eighteen years of age, amiable in his
personal character, and not without titles to respect in his 5
public character as a sovereign prince. In times more
peaceable, and amongst a people more entirely civilized
or more humanized by religion, it is even probable that
he might have discharged his high duties with considerable
distinction; but his lot was thrown upon stormy 10
times, and a most difficult crisis amongst tribes whose
native ferocity was exasperated by debasing forms of
superstition, and by a nationality as well as an inflated
conceit of their own merit absolutely unparalleled; whilst
the circumstances of their hard and trying position under 15
the jealous *surveillance* of an irresistible lord paramount,
in the person of the Russian Czar, gave a fiercer edge to
the natural unamiableness of the Kalmuck disposition, and
irritated its gloomier qualities into action under the restless
impulses of suspicion and permanent distrust. No 20
prince could hope for a cordial allegiance from his subjects
or a peaceful reign under the circumstances of the
case; for the dilemma in which a Kalmuck ruler stood
at present was of this nature: *wanting* the support and
sanction of the Czar, he was inevitably too weak from 25
without to command confidence from his subjects or
resistance to his competitors. On the other hand, *with*
this kind of support, and deriving his title in any degree
from the favor of the Imperial Court, he became almost
in that extent an object of hatred at home and within the 30

whole compass of his own territory. He was at once an object of hatred for the past, being a living monument of national independence ignominiously surrendered; and an object of jealousy for the future, as one who had already advertised himself to be a fitting tool for the ultimate purposes (whatsoever those might prove to be) of the Russian Court. Coming himself to the Kalmuck sceptre under the heaviest weight of prejudice from the unfortunate circumstances of his position, it might have been 5 expected that Oubacha would have been pre-eminently an object of detestation; for, besides his known dependence upon the Cabinet of St. Petersburg, the direct line of succession had been set aside, and the principle of inheritance violently suspended, in favor of his own 10 father, so recently as nineteen years before the era of his own accession, consequently within the lively remembrance of the existing generation. He, therefore, almost equally with his father, stood within the full current of the national prejudices, and might have anticipated the 15 most pointed hostility. But it was not so: such are the caprices in human affairs that he was even, in a moderate sense, popular—a benefit which wore the more cheering aspect and the promises of permanence, inasmuch as he owed it exclusively to his personal qualities of kindness 20 and affability, as well as to the beneficence of his government. On the other hand, to balance this unlooked-for prosperity at the outset of his reign, he met with a rival in popular favor—almost a competitor—in the person of Zebek-Dorchi, a prince with considerable pretensions to 25 the throne, and, perhaps it might be said, with equal pretensions. Zebek-Dorchi was a direct descendant of the same royal house as himself, through a different branch. On public grounds, his claim stood, perhaps, on a footing equally good with that of Oubacha, whilst his personal 30 qualities, even in those aspects which seemed to a philosophical observer most odious and repulsive, promised the most effectual aid to the dark purposes of an intriguer or a conspirator, and were generally fitted to win a popular support precisely in those points where Oubacha was most defective. He was much superior in external appearance to his rival on the throne, and so far better qualified to win the good opinion of a semi-barbarous

people; whilst his dark intellectual qualities of Machiavelian 5
dissimulation, profound hypocrisy, and perfidy which
knew no touch of remorse, were admirably calculated to
sustain any ground which he might win from the simple-hearted
people with whom he had to deal and from the
frank carelessness of his unconscious competitor. 10

At the very outset of his treacherous career, Zebek-Dorchi
was sagacious enough to perceive that nothing
could be gained by open declaration of hostility to the
reigning prince: the choice had been a deliberate act on
the part of Russia, and Elizabeth Petrowna was not the 15
person to recall her own favors with levity or upon slight
grounds. Openly, therefore, to have declared his enmity
toward his relative on the throne, could have had no effect
but that of arming suspicions against his own ulterior
purposes in a quarter where it was most essential to his 20
interest that, for the present, all suspicions should be
hoodwinked. Accordingly, after much meditation, the
course he took for opening his snares was this:—He
raised a rumor that his own life was in danger from the
plots of several Saissang (that is, Kalmuck nobles), who 25
were leagued together under an oath to assassinate him;
and immediately after, assuming a well-counterfeited alarm,
he fled to Tcherkask, followed by sixty-five tents.
From this place he kept up a correspondence with the
Imperial Court, and, by way of soliciting his cause more 30
effectually, he soon repaired in person to St. Petersburg.
Once admitted to personal conferences with the cabinet,
he found no difficulty in winning over the Russian councils
to a concurrence with some of his political views,
and thus covertly introducing the point of that wedge
which was finally to accomplish his purposes. In particular,
he persuaded the Russian Government to make a
very important alteration in the constitution of the Kalmuck
State Council which in effect reorganized the whole 5
political condition of the state and disturbed the balance
of power as previously adjusted. Of this council—in
the Kalmuck language called Sarga—there were eight
members, called Sargatchi; and hitherto it had been the
custom that these eight members should be entirely subordinate
10

to the Khan; holding, in fact, the ministerial character of secretaries and assistants, but in no respect ranking as co-ordinate authorities. That had produced some inconveniences in former reigns; and it was easy for Zebek-Dorchi to point the jealousy of the Russian 15 Court to others more serious which might arise in future circumstances of war or other contingencies. It was resolved, therefore, to place the Sargatchi henceforward on a footing of perfect independence, and, therefore (as regarded responsibility), on a footing of equality with the 20 Khan. Their independence, however, had respect only to their own sovereign; for toward Russia they were placed in a new attitude of direct duty and accountability by the creation in their favor of small pensions (300 roubles a year), which, however, to a Kalmuck of that 25 day were more considerable than might be supposed, and had a further value as marks of honorary distinction emanating from a great empress. Thus far the purposes of Zebek-Dorchi were served effectually for the moment: but, apparently, it was only for the moment; since, in 30 the further development of his plots, this very dependency upon Russian influence would be the most serious obstacle in his way. There was, however, another point carried, which outweighed all inferior considerations, as it gave him a power of setting aside discretionally whatsoever should arise to disturb his plots: he was himself appointed President and Controller of the Sargatchi. The Russian Court had been aware of his high pretensions 5 by birth, and hoped by this promotion to satisfy the ambition which, in some degree, was acknowledged to be a reasonable passion for any man occupying his situation.

Having thus completely blindfolded the Cabinet of Russia, Zebek-Dorchi proceeded in his new character to 10 fulfil his political mission with the Khan of the Kalmucks. So artfully did he prepare the road for his favorable reception at the court of this prince that he was at once and universally welcomed as a public benefactor. The pensions of the councillors were so much additional wealth 15 poured into the Tartar exchequer; as to the ties of dependency thus created, experience had not yet enlightened

these simple tribes as to that result. And that he himself
should be the chief of these mercenary councillors was so
far from being charged upon Zebek as any offence or any 20
ground of suspicion, that his relative the Khan returned
him hearty thanks for his services, under the belief that
he could have accepted this appointment only with a view
to keep out other and more unwelcome pretenders, who
would not have had the same motives of consanguinity or 25
friendship for executing its duties in a spirit of kindness
to the Kalmucks. The first use which he made of his
new functions about the Khan's person was to attack the
Court of Russia, by a romantic villainy not easily to be
credited, for those very acts of interference with the 30
council which he himself had prompted. This was a
dangerous step: but it was indispensable to his farther
advance upon the gloomy path which he had traced out
for himself. A triple vengeance was what he meditated:
1, upon the Russian Cabinet, for having undervalued his
own pretensions to the throne; 2, upon his amiable rival,
for having supplanted him; and 3, upon all those of the
nobility who had manifested their sense of his weakness
by their neglect or their sense of his perfidious character 5
by their suspicions. Here was a colossal outline of wickedness;
and by one in his situation, feeble (as it might
seem) for the accomplishment of its humblest parts, how
was the total edifice to be reared in its comprehensive
grandeur? He, a worm as he was, could he venture to 10
assail the mighty behemoth of Muscovy, the potentate
who counted three hundred languages around the footsteps
of his throne, and from whose "lion ramp" recoiled
alike "baptized and infidel"—Christendom on the one
side, strong by her intellect and her organization, and the 15
"barbaric East" on the other, with her unnumbered
numbers? The match was a monstrous one; but in its
very monstrosity there lay this germ of encouragement—that
it could not be suspected. The very hopelessness
of the scheme grounded his hope; and he resolved to 20
execute a vengeance which should involve as it were, in
the unity of a well-laid tragic fable, all whom he judged
to be his enemies. That vengeance lay in detaching from
the Russian empire the whole Kalmuck nation and breaking
up that system of intercourse which had thus far been 25

beneficial to both. This last was a consideration which moved him but little. True it was that Russia to the Kalmucks had secured lands and extensive pasturage; true it was that the Kalmucks reciprocally to Russia had furnished a powerful cavalry; but the latter loss would be 30 part of his triumph, and the former might be more than compensated in other climates, under other sovereigns. Here was a scheme which, in its final accomplishment, would avenge him bitterly on the Czarina, and in the course of its accomplishment might furnish him with ample occasions for removing his other enemies. It may be readily supposed, indeed, that he who could deliberately raise his eyes to the Russian autocrat as an antagonist 5 in single duel with himself was not likely to feel much anxiety about Kalmuck enemies of whatever rank. He took his resolution, therefore, sternly and irrevocably, to effect this astonishing translation of an ancient people across the pathless deserts of Central Asia, intersected continually by rapid rivers rarely furnished with bridges, 10 and of which the fords were known only to those who might think it for their interest to conceal them, through many nations inhospitable or hostile: frost and snow around them (from the necessity of commencing their flight in winter), famine in their front, and the sabre, or 15 even the artillery of an offended and mighty empress hanging upon their rear for thousands of miles. But what was to be their final mark—the port of shelter after so fearful a course of wandering? Two things were evident: it must be some power at a great distance from Russia, 20 so as to make return even in that view hopeless, and it must be a power of sufficient rank to insure them protection from any hostile efforts on the part of the Czarina for reclaiming them or for chastising their revolt. Both conditions were united obviously in the person of Kien 25 Long, the reigning Emperor of China, who was further recommended to them by his respect for the head of their religion. To China, therefore, and, as their first rendezvous, to the shadow of the Great Chinese Wall, it was settled by Zebek that they should direct their flight. 30

Next came the question of time—*when* should the flight commence? and, finally, the more delicate question

as to the choice of accomplices. To extend the knowledge
of the conspiracy too far was to insure its betrayal
to the Russian Government. Yet, at some stage of the
preparations, it was evident that a very extensive confidence
must be made, because in no other way could the
mass of the Kalmuck population be persuaded to furnish
their families with the requisite equipments for so long a 5
migration. This critical step, however, it was resolved
to defer up to the latest possible moment, and, at all
events, to make no general communication on the subject
until the time of departure should be definitely
settled. In the meantime, Zebek admitted only three 10
persons to his confidence; of whom Oubacha, the reigning
prince, was almost necessarily one; but him, for his
yielding and somewhat feeble character, he viewed rather
in the light of a tool than as one of his active accomplices.
Those whom (if anybody) he admitted to an unreserved 15
participation in his counsels were two only: the
great Lama among the Kalmucks, and his own father-in-law,
Erempel, a ruling prince of some tribe in the neighborhood
of the Caspian Sea, recommended to his favor
not so much by any strength of talent corresponding to 20
the occasion as by his blind devotion to himself and
his passionate anxiety to promote the elevation of his
daughter and his son-in-law to the throne of a sovereign
prince. A titular prince Zebek already was: but this
dignity, without the substantial accompaniment of a sceptre, 25
seemed but an empty sound to both of these ambitious
rebels. The other accomplice, whose name was
Loosang-Dchaltzan, and whose rank was that of Lama,
or Kalmuck pontiff, was a person of far more distinguished
pretensions; he had something of the same 30
gloomy and terrific pride which marked the character of
Zebek himself, manifesting also the same energy, accompanied
by the same unfaltering cruelty, and a natural
facility of dissimulation even more profound. It was by
this man that the other question was settled as to the
time for giving effect to their designs. His own pontifical
character had suggested to him that, in order to
strengthen their influence with the vast mob of simple-minded 5
men whom they were to lead into a howling
wilderness, after persuading them to lay desolate their

24

own ancient hearths, it was indispensable that they should be able, in cases of extremity, to plead the express sanction of God for their entire enterprise. This could only be done by addressing themselves to the great head of 10 their religion, the Dalai-Lama of Tibet. Him they easily persuaded to countenance their schemes: and an oracle was delivered solemnly at Tibet, to the effect that no ultimate prosperity would attend this great Exodus unless it were pursued through the years of the *tiger* and the 15 *hare*. Now the Kalmuck custom is to distinguish their years by attaching to each a denomination taken from one of twelve animals, the exact order of succession being absolutely fixed, so that the cycle revolves of course through a period of a dozen years. Consequently, if the 20 approaching year of the *tiger* were suffered to escape them, in that case the expedition must be delayed for twelve years more; within which period, even were no other unfavorable changes to arise, it was pretty well foreseen that the Russian Government would take most 25 effectual means for bridling their vagrant propensities by a ring-fence of forts or military posts; to say nothing of the still readier plan for securing their fidelity (a plan already talked of in all quarters) by exacting a large body of hostages selected from the families of the most influential 30 nobles. On these cogent considerations, it was solemnly determined that this terrific experiment should be made in the next year of the *tiger*, which happened to fall upon the Christian year 1771. With respect to the month, there was, unhappily for the Kalmucks, even less latitude allowed to their choice than with respect to the year. It was absolutely necessary, or it was thought so, that the different divisions of the nation, which pastured their flocks on both banks of the Wolga, should have the 5 means of effecting an instantaneous junction, because the danger of being intercepted by flying columns of the imperial armies was precisely the greatest at the outset. Now, from the want of bridges or sufficient river craft for transporting so vast a body of men, the sole means 10 which could be depended upon (especially where so many women, children, and camels were concerned) was *ice*; and this, in a state of sufficient firmness, could not be absolutely counted upon before the month of January.

Hence it happened that this astonishing Exodus of a 15
whole nation, before so much as a whisper of the design
had begun to circulate amongst those whom it most interested,
before it was even suspected that any man's wishes
pointed in that direction, had been definitely appointed
for January of the year 1771. And almost up to the 20
Christmas of 1770 the poor simple Kalmuck herdsmen
and their families were going nightly to their peaceful
beds without even dreaming that the *fiat* had already
gone forth from their rulers which consigned those quiet
abodes, together with the peace and comfort which reigned 25
within them, to a withering desolation, now close at
hand.

Meantime war raged on a great scale between Russia
and the Sultan; and, until the time arrived for throwing
off their vassalage, it was necessary that Oubacha should 30
contribute his usual contingent of martial aid. Nay, it
had unfortunately become prudent that he should contribute
much more than his usual aid. Human experience
gives ample evidence that in some mysterious and
unaccountable way no great design is ever agitated, no
matter how few or how faithful may be the participators,
but that some presentiment—some dim misgiving—is
kindled amongst those whom it is chiefly important to
blind. And, however it might have happened, certain it 5
is that already, when as yet no syllable of the conspiracy
had been breathed to any man whose very existence was
not staked upon its concealment, nevertheless some vague
and uneasy jealousy had arisen in the Russian Cabinet
as to the future schemes of the Kalmuck Khan: and 10
very probable it is that, but for the war then raging, and
the consequent prudence of conciliating a very important
vassal, or, at least, of abstaining from what would powerfully
alienate him, even at that moment such measures
would have been adopted as must forever have intercepted 15
the Kalmuck schemes. Slight as were the jealousies
of the Imperial Court, they had not escaped the
Machiavelian eyes of Zebek and the Lama. And under
their guidance, Oubacha, bending to the circumstances of
the moment, and meeting the jealousy of the Russian 20
Court with a policy corresponding to their own, strove by

unusual zeal to efface the Czarina's unfavorable impressions.
He enlarged the scale of his contributions, and
that so prodigiously that he absolutely carried to headquarters
a force of 35,000 cavalry, fully equipped: some 25
go further, and rate the amount beyond 40,000; but the
smaller estimate is, at all events, *within* the truth.

With this magnificent array of cavalry, heavy as well as
light, the Khan went into the field under great expectations;
and these he more than realized. Having the 30
good fortune to be concerned with so ill-organized and
disorderly a description of force as that which at all times
composed the bulk of a Turkish army, he carried victory
along with his banners; gained many partial successes;
and at last, in a pitched battle, overthrew the Turkish
force opposed to him, with a loss of 5000 men left upon
the field.

These splendid achievements seemed likely to operate
in various ways against the impending revolt. Oubacha 5
had now a strong motive, in the martial glory acquired,
for continuing his connection with the empire in whose
service he had won it, and by whom only it could be fully
appreciated. He was now a great marshal of a great
empire, one of the Paladins around the imperial throne; 10
in China he would be nobody, or (worse than that) a mendicant
alien, prostrate at the feet, and soliciting the precarious
alms, of a prince with whom he had no connection.
Besides, it might reasonably be expected that the Czarina,
grateful for the really efficient aid given by the Tartar 15
prince, would confer upon him such eminent rewards as
might be sufficient to anchor his hopes upon Russia, and
to wean him from every possible seduction. These were
the obvious suggestions of prudence and good sense to
every man who stood neutral in the case. But they were 20
disappointed. The Czarina knew her obligations to the
Khan, but she did not acknowledge them. Wherefore?
That is a mystery perhaps never to be explained. So it
was, however. The Khan went unhonored; no *ukase*
ever proclaimed his merits; and, perhaps, had he even 25
been abundantly recompensed by Russia, there were
others who would have defeated these tendencies to
reconciliation. Erempel, Zebek, and Loosang the Lama

were pledged life-deep to prevent any accommodation; and their efforts were unfortunately seconded by those of 30 their deadliest enemies. In the Russian Court there were at that time some great nobles preoccupied with feelings of hatred and blind malice toward the Kalmucks quite as strong as any which the Kalmucks could harbor toward Russia, and not, perhaps, so well founded. Just as much as the Kalmucks hated the Russian yoke, their galling assumption of authority, the marked air of disdain, as toward a nation of ugly, stupid, and filthy barbarians, which too generally marked the Russian bearing and 5 language, but, above all, the insolent contempt, or even outrages, which the Russian governors or great military commandants tolerated in their followers toward the barbarous religion and superstitious mummeries of the Kalmuck priesthood—precisely in that extent did the ferocity 10 of the Russian resentment, and their wrath at seeing the trampled worm turn or attempt a feeble retaliation, react upon the unfortunate Kalmucks. At this crisis, it is probable that envy and wounded pride, upon witnessing the splendid victories of Oubacha and Momotbacha over the 15 Turks and Bashkirs, contributed strength to the Russian irritation. And it must have been through the intrigues of those nobles about her person who chiefly smarted under these feelings that the Czarina could ever have lent herself to the unwise and ungrateful policy pursued 20 at this critical period toward the Kalmuck Khan. That Czarina was no longer Elizabeth Petrowna; it was Catharine II.—a princess who did not often err so injuriously (injuriously for herself as much as for others) in the measures of her government. She had soon ample reason for 25 repenting of her false policy. Meantime, how much it must have co-operated with the other motives previously acting upon Oubacha in sustaining his determination to revolt, and how powerfully it must have assisted the efforts of all the Tartar chieftains in preparing the minds of their 30 people to feel the necessity of this difficult enterprise, by arming their pride and their suspicions against the Russian Government, through the keenness of their sympathy with the wrongs of their insulted prince, may be readily imagined. It is a fact, and it has been confessed by candid Russians themselves when treating of this great dismemberment, that the conduct of the Russian Cabinet throughout the period of suspense, and during the crisis of hesitation in the Kalmuck Council, was exactly such 5 as was most desirable for the purposes of the conspirators; it was such, in fact, as to set the seal to all their machinations, by supplying distinct evidences and official vouchers for what could otherwise have been at the most matters of doubtful suspicion and indirect presumption. 10

Nevertheless, in the face of all these arguments, and even allowing their weight so far as not at all to deny the injustice or the impolicy of the imperial ministers, it is contended by many persons who have reviewed the affair with a command of all the documents bearing on the case, 15 more especially the letters or minutes of council subsequently discovered in the handwriting of Zebek-Dorchi, and the important evidence of the Russian captive, Weseloff, who was carried off by the Kalmucks in their flight, that beyond all doubt Oubacha was powerless for any 20 purpose of impeding or even of delaying the revolt. He himself, indeed, was under religious obligations of the most terrific solemnity never to flinch from the enterprise or even to slacken in his zeal; for Zebek-Dorchi, distrusting the firmness of his resolution under any unusual 25 pressure of alarm or difficulty, had, in the very earliest stage of the conspiracy, availed himself of the Khan's well-known superstition, to engage him, by means of previous concert with the priests and their head, the Lama, in some dark and mysterious rites of consecration, terminating 30 in oaths under such terrific sanctions as no Kalmuck would have courage to violate. As far, therefore, as regarded the personal share of the Khan in what was to come, Zebek was entirely at his ease; he knew him to be so deeply pledged by religious terrors to the prosecution of the conspiracy that no honors within the Czarina's gift could have possibly shaken his adhesion; and then, as to threats from the same quarter, he knew him to be sealed against those fears by others of a gloomier character, 5 and better adapted to his peculiar temperament. For Oubacha was a brave man, as respected all bodily enemies or the dangers of human warfare, but was as sensitive and timid as the most superstitious of old women in

facing the frowns of a priest or under the vague anticipations 10
of ghostly retributions. But had it been otherwise,
and had there been any reason to apprehend an unsteady
demeanor on the part of this prince at the approach
of the critical moment, such were the changes already
effected in the state of their domestic politics amongst 15
the Tartars by the undermining arts of Zebek-Dorchi, and
his ally the Lama, that very little importance would have
attached to that doubt. All power was now effectually
lodged in the hands of Zebek-Dorchi. He was the true
and absolute wielder of the Kalmuck sceptre; all measures 20
of importance were submitted to his discretion, and
nothing was finally resolved but under his dictation.
This result he had brought about, in a year or two, by
means sufficiently simple: first of all, by availing himself
of the prejudice in his favor, so largely diffused amongst 25
the lowest of the Kalmucks, that his own title to the
throne in quality of great-grandson in a direct line from
Ajouka, the most illustrious of all the Kalmuck Khans,
stood upon a better basis than that of Oubacha, who
derived from a collateral branch; secondly, with respect 30
to the sole advantage which Oubacha possessed above
himself in the ratification of his title, by improving this
difference between their situations to the disadvantage
of his competitor, as one who had not scrupled to accept
that triumph from an alien power at the price of his independence,
which he himself (as he would have it understood)
disdained to court; thirdly, by his own talents
and address, coupled with the ferocious energy of his
moral character; fourthly—and perhaps in an equal 5
degree—by the criminal facility and good nature of
Oubacha; finally (which is remarkable enough, as illustrating
the character of the man), by that very new modelling
of the Sarga, or Privy Council, which he had used
as a principal topic of abuse and malicious insinuation 10
against the Russian Government, whilst, in reality, he
first had suggested the alteration to the Empress, and
he chiefly appropriated the political advantages which it
was fitted to yield. For, as he was himself appointed the
chief of the Sargatchi, and as the pensions of the inferior 15
Sargatchi passed through his hands, whilst in effect they
owed their appointments to his nomination, it may be

easily supposed that, whatever power existed in the state
capable of controlling the Khan, being held by the Sarga
under its new organization, and this body being completely 20
under his influence, the final result was to throw
all the functions of the state, whether nominally in the
prince or in the council, substantially into the hands of
this one man; whilst, at the same time, from the strict
league which he maintained with the Lama, all the thunders 25
of the spiritual power were always ready to come in
aid of the magistrate, or to supply his incapacity in cases
which he could not reach.

But the time was now rapidly approaching for the
mighty experiment. The day was drawing near on which 30
the signal was to be given for raising the standard of
revolt, and, by a combined movement on both sides of the
Wolga, for spreading the smoke of one vast conflagration
that should wrap in a common blaze their own huts and
the stately cities of their enemies over the breadth and
length of those great provinces in which their flocks were
dispersed. The year of the *tiger* was now within one
little month of its commencement; the fifth morning of
that year was fixed for the fatal day when the fortunes 5
and happiness of a whole nation were to be put upon the
hazard of a dicer's throw; and as yet that nation was in
profound ignorance of the whole plan. The Khan, such
was the kindness of his nature, could not bring himself to
make the revelation so urgently required. It was clear, 10
however, that this could not be delayed; and Zebek-Dorchi
took the task willingly upon himself. But where
or how should this notification be made, so as to exclude
Russian hearers? After some deliberation the following
plan was adopted:—Couriers, it was contrived, should 15
arrive in furious haste, one upon the heels of another,
reporting a sudden inroad of the Kirghises and Bashkirs
upon the Kalmuck lands, at a point distant about 120
miles. Thither all the Kalmuck families, according to
immemorial custom, were required to send a separate
representative; 20
and there, accordingly, within three days, all
appeared. The distance, the solitary ground appointed
for the rendezvous, the rapidity of the march, all tended

to make it almost certain that no Russian could be
present. Zebek-Dorchi then came forward. He did 25
not waste many words upon rhetoric. He unfurled an
immense sheet of parchment, visible from the outermost
distance at which any of this vast crowd could stand;
the total number amounted to 80,000; all saw, and many heard.
They were told of the oppressions of Russia; 30
of her pride and haughty disdain, evidenced toward them
by a thousand acts; of her contempt for their religion;
of her determination to reduce them to absolute slavery;
of the preliminary measures she had already taken by
erecting forts upon many of the great rivers of their neighborhood;
of the ulterior intentions she thus announced
to circumscribe their pastoral lands, until they would all
be obliged to renounce their flocks, and to collect in
towns like Sarepta, there to pursue mechanical and servile 5
trades of shoemaker, tailor, and weaver, such as the free-born
Tartar had always disdained. "Then again," said
the subtle prince, "she increases her military levies upon
our population every year. We pour out our blood as
young men in her defence, or, more often, in support of 10
her insolent aggressions; and, as old men, we reap nothing
from our sufferings nor benefit by our survivorship
where so many are sacrificed." At this point of his
harangue Zebek produced several papers (forged, as it is
generally believed, by himself and the Lama), containing 15
projects of the Russian Court for a general transfer of
the eldest sons, taken *en masse* from the greatest Kalmuck
families, to the Imperial Court. "Now, let this be once
accomplished," he argued, "and there is an end of all
useful resistance from that day forwards. Petitions we 20
might make, or even remonstrances; as men of words,
we might play a bold part; but for deeds; for that sort
of language by which our ancestors were used to speak—holding
us by such a chain, Russia would make a jest of
our wishes, knowing full well that we should not dare to 25
make any effectual movement."

Having thus sufficiently roused the angry passions of his
vast audience, and having alarmed their fears by this
pretended scheme against their firstborn (an artifice
which was indispensable to his purpose, because it met 30

beforehand *every* form of amendment to his proposal
coming from the more moderate nobles, who would not
otherwise have failed to insist upon trying the effect of
bold addresses to the Empress before resorting to any
desperate extremity), Zebek-Dorchi opened his scheme of
revolt, and, if so, of instant revolt; since any preparations
reported at St. Petersburg would be a signal for the
armies of Russia to cross into such positions from all
parts of Asia as would effectually intercept their march. 5
It is remarkable, however, that with all his audacity and
his reliance upon the momentary excitement of the Kalmucks,
the subtle prince did not venture, at this stage of
his seduction, to make so startling a proposal as that of
a flight to China. All that he held out for the present 10
was a rapid march to the Temba or some other great
river, which they were to cross, and to take up a strong
position on the farther bank, from which, as from a post
of conscious security, they could hold a bolder language
to the Czarina, and one which would have a better chance 15
of winning a favorable audience.

   These things, in the irritated condition of the simple
Tartars, passed by acclamation; and all returned homeward
to push forward with the most furious speed the
preparations for their awful undertaking. Rapid and 20
energetic these of necessity were; and in that degree
they became noticeable and manifest to the Russians who
happened to be intermingled with the different hordes,
either on commercial errands, or as agents officially from
the Russian Government, some in a financial, others in a 25
diplomatic character.

   Among these last (indeed, at the head of them) was a
Russian of some distinction, by name Kichinskoi—a man
memorable for his vanity, and memorable also as one of
the many victims to the Tartar revolution. This Kichinskoi 30
had been sent by the Empress as her envoy to overlook
the conduct of the Kalmucks. He was styled the
Grand Pristaw, or Great Commissioner, and was universally
known amongst the Tartar tribes by this title. His
mixed character of ambassador and of political *surveillant*,
combined with the dependent state of the Kalmucks,
gave him a real weight in the Tartar councils, and might

have given him a far greater had not his outrageous
self-conceit and his arrogant confidence in his own 5
authority, as due chiefly to his personal qualities for
command, led him into such harsh displays of power,
and menaces so odious to the Tartar pride, as very soon
made him an object of their profoundest malice. He had
publicly insulted the Khan; and, upon making a communication
10
to him to the effect that some reports began to
circulate, and even to reach the Empress, of a design in
agitation to fly from the imperial dominions, he had ventured
to say, "But this you dare not attempt; I laugh at
such rumors; yes, Khan, I laugh at them to the Empress; 15
for you are a chained bear, and that you know." The
Khan turned away on his heel with marked disdain; and
the Pristaw, foaming at the mouth, continued to utter,
amongst those of the Khan's attendants who stayed
behind to catch his real sentiments in a moment of unguarded 20
passion, all that the blindest frenzy of rage could
suggest to the most presumptuous of fools. It was now
ascertained that suspicion *had* arisen; but, at the same
time, it was ascertained that the Pristaw spoke no more
than the truth in representing himself to have discredited 25
these suspicions. The fact was that the mere infatuation
of vanity made him believe that nothing could go on undetected
by his all-piercing sagacity, and that no rebellion
could prosper when rebuked by his commanding presence.
The Tartars, therefore, pursued their preparations, confiding 30
in the obstinate blindness of the Grand Pristaw as
in their perfect safeguard, and such it proved—to his
own ruin as well as that of myriads beside.

Christmas arrived; and, a little before that time, courier
upon courier came dropping in, one upon the very heels
of another, to St. Petersburg, assuring the Czarina that
beyond all doubt the Kalmucks were in the very crisis of
departure. These dispatches came from the Governor
of Astrachan, and copies were instantly forwarded to 5
Kichinskoi. Now, it happened that between this governor—a
Russian named Beketoff—and the Pristaw
had been an ancient feud. The very name of Beketoff
inflamed his resentment; and no sooner did he see that

hated name attached to the dispatch than he felt himself 10
confirmed in his former views with tenfold bigotry, and
wrote instantly, in terms of the most pointed ridicule,
against the new alarmist, pledging his own head upon the
visionariness of his alarms. Beketoff, however, was not
to be put down by a few hard words, or by ridicule: he 15
persisted in his statements; the Russian ministry were
confounded by the obstinacy of the disputants; and some
were beginning even to treat the Governor of Astrachan
as a bore, and as the dupe of his own nervous terrors,
when the memorable day arrived, the fatal 5th of January, 20
which forever terminated the dispute and put a seal upon
the earthly hopes and fortunes of unnumbered myriads.
The Governor of Astrachan was the first to hear the news.
Stung by the mixed furies of jealousy, of triumphant
vengeance, and of anxious ambition, he sprang into his 25
sledge, and, at the rate of 300 miles a day, pursued his
route to St. Petersburg—rushed into the Imperial presence—
announced
the total realization of his worst predictions;
and, upon the confirmation of this intelligence
by subsequent dispatches from many different posts on 30
the Wolga, he received an imperial commission to seize
the person of his deluded enemy and to keep him in strict
captivity. These orders were eagerly fulfilled; and the
unfortunate Kichinskoi soon afterwards expired of grief
and mortification in the gloomy solitude of a dungeon—a
victim to his own immeasurable vanity and the blinding
self-delusions of a presumption that refused all warning.

   The Governor of Astrachan had been but too faithful
a prophet. Perhaps even *he* was surprised at the suddenness 5
with which the verification followed his reports.
Precisely on the 5th of January, the day so solemnly
appointed under religious sanctions by the Lama, the
Kalmucks on the east bank of the Wolga were seen at
the earliest dawn of day assembling by troops and 10
squadrons and in the tumultuous movement of some great
morning of battle. Tens of thousands continued moving
off the ground at every half hour's interval. Women
and children, to the amount of two hundred thousand and
upward, were placed upon wagons or upon camels, and 15

drew off by masses of twenty thousand at once—placed
under suitable escorts, and continually swelled in numbers
by other outlying bodies of the horde,—who kept falling
in at various distances upon the first and second day's
march. From sixty to eighty thousand of those who 20
were the best mounted stayed behind the rest of the
tribes, with purposes of devastation and plunder more
violent than prudence justified or the amiable character
of the Khan could be supposed to approve. But in this,
as in other instances, he was completely overruled by the 25
malignant counsels of Zebek-Dorchi. The first tempest
of the desolating fury of the Tartars discharged itself
upon their own habitations. But this, as cutting off all
infirm looking backward from the hardships of their
march, had been thought so necessary a measure by all 30
the chieftains that even Oubacha himself was the first to
authorize the act by his own example. He seized a torch
previously prepared with materials the most durable as
well as combustible, and steadily applied it to the timbers
of his own palace. Nothing was saved from the general
wreck except the portable part of the domestic utensils
and that part of the woodwork which could be applied
to the manufacture of the long Tartar lances. This
chapter in their memorable day's work being finished, 5
and the whole of their villages throughout a district of
ten thousand square miles in one simultaneous blaze, the
Tartars waited for further orders.

These, it was intended, should have taken a character of
valedictory vengeance, and thus have left behind to the 10
Czarina a dreadful commentary upon the main motives
of their flight. It was the purpose of Zebek-Dorchi that
all the Russian towns, churches, and buildings of every
description should be given up to pillage and destruction,
and such treatment applied to the defenceless inhabitants 15
as might naturally be expected from a fierce people
already infuriated by the spectacle of their own outrages,
and by the bloody retaliations which they must necessarily
have provoked. This part of the tragedy, however, was
happily intercepted by a providential disappointment at 20
the very crisis of departure. It has been mentioned
already that the motive for selecting the depth of winter

as the season of flight (which otherwise was obviously
the very worst possible) had been the impossibility of
effecting a junction sufficiently rapid with the tribes on 25
the west of the Wolga, in the absence of bridges, unless
by a natural bridge of ice. For this one advantage the
Kalmuck leaders had consented to aggravate by a thousand-fold
the calamities inevitable to a rapid flight over
boundless tracts of country with women, children, and 30
herds of cattle—for this one single advantage; and yet,
after all, it was lost. The reason never has been explained
satisfactorily, but the fact was such. Some have said
that the signals were not properly concerted for marking
the moment of absolute departure—that is, for signifying
whether the settled intention of the Eastern Kalmucks
might not have been suddenly interrupted by adverse
intelligence. Others have supposed that the ice might
not be equally strong on both sides of the river, and 5
might even be generally insecure for the treading of
heavy and heavily laden animals such as camels. But
the prevailing notion is that some accidental movements
on the 3d and 4th of January of Russian troops in the
neighborhood of the Western Kalmucks, though really 10
having no reference to them or their plans, had been construed
into certain signs that all was discovered, and that
the prudence of the Western chieftains, who, from situation,
had never been exposed to those intrigues by which
Zebek-Dorchi had practised upon the pride of the Eastern 15
tribes, now stepped in to save their people from ruin.
Be the cause what it might, it is certain that the Western
Kalmucks were in some way prevented from forming the
intended junction with their brethren of the opposite
bank; and the result was that at least one hundred 20
thousand of these Tartars were left behind in Russia.
This accident it was which saved their Russian neighbors
universally from the desolation which else awaited them.
One general massacre and conflagration would assuredly
have surprised them, to the utter extermination of their 25
property, their houses, and themselves, had it not been
for this disappointment. But the Eastern chieftains did
not dare to put to hazard the safety of their brethren
under the first impulse of the Czarina's vengeance for so
dreadful a tragedy; for, as they were well aware of too many 30

circumstances by which she might discover the concurrence of the Western people in the general scheme of revolt, they justly feared that she would thence infer their concurrence also in the bloody events which marked its outset.

Little did the Western Kalmucks guess what reasons they also had for gratitude, on account of an interposition so unexpected, and which at the moment they so generally deplored. Could they but have witnessed the thousandth part of the sufferings which overtook their Eastern brethren 5 in the first month of their sad flight, they would have blessed Heaven for their own narrow escape; and yet these sufferings of the first month were but a prelude or foretaste comparatively slight of those which afterward succeeded. 10

For now began to unroll the most awful series of calamities, and the most extensive, which is anywhere recorded to have visited the sons and daughters of men. It is possible that the sudden inroads of destroying nations, such as the Huns, or the Avars, or the Mongol 15 Tartars, may have inflicted misery as extensive; but there the misery and the desolation would be sudden, like the flight of volleying lightning. Those who were spared at first would generally be spared to the end; those who perished would perish instantly. It is possible that the 20 French retreat from Moscow may have made some nearer approach to this calamity in duration, though still a feeble and miniature approach; for the French sufferings did not commence in good earnest until about one month from the time of leaving Moscow; and though it is true 25 that afterward the vials of wrath were emptied upon the devoted army for six or seven weeks in succession, yet what is that to this Kalmuck tragedy, which lasted for more than as many months? But the main feature of horror, by which the Tartar march was distinguished from 30 the French, lies in the accompaniment of women[5] and children. There were both, it is true, with the French army, but so few as to bear no visible proportion to the total numbers concerned. The French, in short, were merely an army—a host of professional destroyers, whose regular trade was bloodshed, and whose regular element 5 was danger and suffering. But the Tartars were a nation

carrying along with them more than two hundred and
fifty thousand women and children, utterly unequal, for
the most part, to any contest with the calamities before
them. The Children of Israel were in the same circumstances 10
as to the accompaniment of their families; but
they were released from the pursuit of their enemies in a
very early stage of their flight; and their subsequent residence
in the Desert was not a march, but a continued halt
and under a continued interposition of Heaven for their 15
comfortable support. Earthquakes, again, however comprehensive
in their ravages, are shocks of a moment's
duration. A much nearer approach made to the wide
range and the long duration of the Kalmuck tragedy may
have been in a pestilence such as that which visited 20
Athens in the Peloponnesian war, or London in the reign
of Charles II. There, also, the martyrs were counted by
myriads, and the period of the desolation was counted
by months. But, after all, the total amount of destruction
was on a smaller scale; and there was this feature of 25
alleviation to the *conscious* pressure of the calamity—that
the misery was withdrawn from public notice into private
chambers and hospitals. The siege of Jerusalem by
Vespasian and his son, taken in its entire circumstances,
comes nearest of all—for breadth and depth of suffering, 30
for duration, for the exasperation of the suffering from
without by internal feuds, and, finally, for that last most
appalling expression of the furnace heat of the anguish in
its power to extinguish the natural affections even of
maternal love. But, after all, each case had circumstances
of romantic misery peculiar to itself—circumstances 5
without precedent, and (wherever human nature is ennobled
by Christianity), it may be confidently hoped, never
to be repeated.

   The first point to be reached, before any hope of repose
could be encouraged, was the River Jaik. This was not 10
above 300 miles from the main point of departure on the
Wolga; and, if the march thither was to be a forced one
and a severe one, it was alleged, on the other hand, that
the suffering would be the more brief and transient;
one summary exertion, not to be repeated, and all was 15
achieved. Forced the march was, and severe beyond

example: there the forewarning proved correct; but the
promised rest proved a mere phantom of the wilderness—a
visionary rainbow, which fled before their hope-sick
eyes, across these interminable solitudes, for seven months 20
of hardship and calamity, without a pause. These sufferings,
by their very nature and the circumstances under
which they arose, were (like the scenery of the steppes)
somewhat monotonous in their coloring and external
features; what variety, however, there was, will be most 25
naturally exhibited by tracing historically the successive
stages of the general misery exactly as it unfolded itself
under the double agency of weakness still increasing from
within and hostile pressure from without. Viewed in this
manner, under the real order of development, it is remarkable 30
that these sufferings of the Tartars, though under
the moulding hands of accident, arrange themselves
almost with a scenical propriety. They seem combined
as with the skill of an artist; the intensity of the misery
advancing regularly with the advances of the march, and
the stages of the calamity corresponding to the stages
of the route; so that, upon raising the curtain which
veils the great catastrophe, we behold one vast climax of
anguish, towering upward by regular gradations as if constructed
5
artificially for picturesque effect—a result which
might not have been surprising had it been reasonable to
anticipate the same rate of speed, and even an accelerated
rate, as prevailing through the latter stages of the expedition.
But it seemed, on the contrary, most reasonable to 10
calculate upon a continual decrement in the rate of motion
according to the increasing distance from the headquarters
of the pursuing enemy. This calculation, however, was
defeated by the extraordinary circumstance that the Russian
armies did not begin to close in very fiercely upon 15
the Kalmucks until after they had accomplished a distance
of full 2000 miles: 1000 miles farther on the assaults
became even more tumultuous and murderous: and already
the great shadows of the Chinese Wall were dimly descried,
when the frenzy and *acharnement* of the pursuers and the 20
bloody desperation of the miserable fugitives had reached
its uttermost extremity. Let us briefly rehearse the main
stages of the misery and trace the ascending steps of the

tragedy, according to the great divisions of the route marked out by the central rivers of Asia. 25

The first stage, we have already said, was from the Wolga to the Jaik; the distance about 300 miles; the time allowed seven days. For the first week, therefore, the rate of marching averaged about 43 English miles a day. The weather was cold, but bracing; and, at a more 30 moderate pace, this part of the journey might have been accomplished without much distress by a people as hardy as the Kalmucks: as it was, the cattle suffered greatly from overdriving; milk began to fail even for the children; the sheep perished by wholesale; and the children themselves were saved only by the innumerable camels.

The Cossacks who dwelt upon the banks of the Jaik were the first among the subjects of Russia to come into collision with the Kalmucks. Great was their surprise at 5 the suddenness of the irruption, and great also their consternation; for, according to their settled custom, by far the greater part of their number was absent during the winter months at the fisheries upon the Caspian. Some who were liable to surprise at the most exposed points 10 fled in crowds to the fortress of Koulagina, which was immediately invested and summoned by Oubacha. He had, however, in his train only a few light pieces of artillery; and the Russian commandant at Koulagina, being aware of the hurried circumstances in which the 15 Khan was placed, and that he stood upon the very edge, as it were, of a renewed flight, felt encouraged by these considerations to a more obstinate resistance than might else have been advisable with an enemy so little disposed to observe the usages of civilized warfare. The period of 20 his anxiety was not long. On the fifth day of the siege he descried from the walls a succession of Tartar couriers, mounted upon fleet Bactrian camels, crossing the vast plains around the fortress at a furious pace and riding into the Kalmuck encampment at various points. 25 Great agitation appeared immediately to follow: orders were soon after dispatched in all directions; and it became speedily known that upon a distant flank of the Kalmuck movement a bloody and exterminating battle had been fought the day before, in which one entire tribe of the 30

41

Khan's dependents, numbering not less than 9000 fighting men, had perished to the last man. This was the *ouloss*, or clan, called Feka-Zechorr, between whom and the Cossacks there was a feud of ancient standing. In selecting, therefore, the points of attack, on occasion of the present hasty inroad, the Cossack chiefs were naturally eager so to direct their efforts as to combine with the service of the Empress some gratification to their own party hatreds, more especially as the present was likely 5 to be their final opportunity for revenge if the Kalmuck evasion should prosper. Having, therefore, concentrated as large a body of Cossack cavalry as circumstances allowed, they attacked the hostile *ouloss* with a precipitation which denied to it all means for communicating with 10 Oubacha; for the necessity of commanding an ample range of pasturage, to meet the necessities of their vast flocks and herds, had separated this *ouloss* from the Khan's headquarters by an interval of 80 miles; and thus it was, and not from oversight, that it came to be thrown entirely 15 upon its own resources. These had proved insufficient: retreat, from the exhausted state of their horses and camels, no less than from the prodigious encumbrances of their live stock, was absolutely out of the question: quarter was disdained on the one side, and would not 20 have been granted on the other: and thus it had happened that the setting sun of that one day (the thirteenth from the first opening of the revolt) threw his parting rays upon the final agonies of an ancient *ouloss*, stretched upon a bloody field, who on that day's dawning had held and 25 styled themselves an independent nation.

Universal consternation was diffused through the wide borders of the Khan's encampment by this disastrous intelligence, not so much on account of the numbers slain, or the total extinction of a powerful ally, as because 30 the position of the Cossack force was likely to put to hazard the future advances of the Kalmucks, or at least to retard and hold them in check until the heavier columns of the Russian army should arrive upon their flanks. The siege of Koulagina was instantly raised; and that signal, so fatal to the happiness of the women and their children, once again resounded through the tents—the signal for flight, and this time for a flight more rapid than ever. About 150 miles ahead of their present position, there arose a tract of hilly country, forming a sort of margin to the vast, sealike expanse of champaign savannas, steppes, and occasionally of sandy deserts, which stretched away on each side of this margin both eastwards and westwards. Pretty nearly in the centre of this hilly range lay a narrow defile, through which passed the nearest and the most practicable route to the River Torgau (the farther bank of which river offered the next great station of security for a general halt). It was the more essential to gain this pass before the Cossacks, inasmuch as not only would the delay in forcing the pass give time to the Russian pursuing columns for combining their attacks and for bringing up their artillery, but also because (even if all enemies in pursuit were thrown out of the question) it was held, by those best acquainted with the difficult and obscure geography of these pathless steppes—that the loss of this one narrow strait amongst the hills would have the effect of throwing them (as their only alternative in a case where so wide a sweep of pasturage was required) upon a circuit of at least 500 miles extra; besides that, after all, this circuitous route would carry them to the Torgau at a point unfitted for the passage of their heavy baggage. The defile in the hills, therefore, it was resolved to gain; and yet, unless they moved upon it with the velocity of light cavalry, there was little chance but it would be found preoccupied by the Cossacks. They, it is true, had suffered greatly in the recent sanguinary action with the defeated *ouloss*; but the excitement of victory, and the intense sympathy with their unexampled triumph, had again swelled their ranks, and would probably act with the force of a vortex to draw in their simple countrymen from the Caspian. The question, therefore, of preoccupation was reduced to a race. The Cossacks were marching upon an oblique line not above 50 miles longer than that which led to the same point from the Kalmuck headquarters before Koulagina; and therefore, without the most furious haste on the part of the Kalmucks, there was not a chance for them, burdened and "trashed"[6] as they were, to anticipate so agile a light cavalry as the

Cossacks in seizing this important pass.

Dreadful were the feelings of the poor women on hearing this exposition of the case. For they easily understood that too capital an interest (the *summa rerum*) 15 was now at stake to allow of any regard to minor interests, or what would be considered such in their present circumstances. The dreadful week already passed—their inauguration in misery—was yet fresh in their remembrance. The scars of suffering were impressed 20 not only upon their memories, but upon their very persons and the persons of their children; and they knew that, where no speed had much chance of meeting the cravings of the chieftains, no test would be accepted, short of absolute exhaustion, that as much had been accomplished 25 as could be accomplished. Weseloff, the Russian captive, has recorded the silent wretchedness with which the women and elder boys assisted in drawing the tent ropes. On the 5th of January all had been animation and the joyousness of indefinite expectation; now, on the contrary, 30 a brief but bitter experience had taught them to take an amended calculation of what it was that lay before them.

One whole day and far into the succeeding night had
the renewed flight continued; the sufferings had been 5
greater than before, for the cold had been more intense,
and many perished out of the living creatures through
every class except only the camels—whose powers of
endurance seemed equally adapted to cold and heat.
The second morning, however, brought an alleviation to 10
the distress. Snow had begun to fall; and, though not
deep at present, it was easily foreseen that it soon would
be so, and that, as a halt would in that case become
unavoidable, no plan could be better than that of staying
where they were, especially as the same cause would 15
check the advance of the Cossacks. Here, then, was the
last interval of comfort which gleamed upon the unhappy
nation during their whole migration. For ten days the
snow continued to fall with little intermission. At the
end of that time, keen, bright, frosty weather succeeded; 20
the drifting had ceased. In three days the smooth expanse
became firm enough to support the treading of the
camels; and the flight was recommenced. But during
the halt much domestic comfort had been enjoyed; and,
for the last time, universal plenty. The cows and oxen 25
had perished in such vast numbers on the previous
marches that an order was now issued to turn what
remained to account by slaughtering the whole, and
salting whatever part should be found to exceed the
immediate consumption. This measure led to a scene 30
of general banqueting, and even of festivity amongst all
who were not incapacitated for joyous emotions by distress
of mind, by grief for the unhappy experience of the
few last days, and by anxiety for the too gloomy future.
Seventy thousand persons of all ages had already perished,
exclusively of the many thousand allies who had been cut
down by the Cossack sabre. And the losses in reversion
were likely to be many more. For rumors began now to
arrive from all quarters, by the mounted couriers whom 5
the Khan had dispatched to the rear and to each flank as
well as in advance, that large masses of the imperial troops
were converging from all parts of Central Asia to the fords
of the River Torgau, as the most convenient point for
intercepting the flying tribes; and it was already well 10

known that a powerful division was close in their rear, and was retarded only by the numerous artillery which had been judged necessary to support their operations. New motives were thus daily arising for quickening the motions of the wretched Kalmucks, and for exhausting those who were previously but too much exhausted.

It was not until the 2d day of February that the Khan's advanced guard came in sight of Ouchim, the defile among the hills of Moulgaldchares, in which they anticipated so bloody an opposition from the Cossacks. A pretty large body of these light cavalry had, in fact, preoccupied the pass by some hours; but the Khan, having two great advantages—namely, a strong body of infantry, who had been conveyed by sections of five on about two hundred camels, and some pieces of light artillery which he had not yet been forced to abandon—soon began to make a serious impression upon this unsupported detachment; and they would probably at any rate have retired; but, at the very moment when they were making some dispositions in that view, Zebek-Dorchi appeared upon their rear with a body of trained riflemen, who had distinguished themselves in the war with Turkey. These men had contrived to crawl unobserved over the cliffs which skirted the ravine, availing themselves of the dry beds of the summer torrents and other inequalities of the ground to conceal their movement. Disorder and trepidation ensued instantly in the Cossack files; the Khan, who had been waiting with the *élite* of his heavy cavalry, charged furiously upon them. Total overthrow followed to the Cossacks, and a slaughter such as in some measure avenged the recent bloody extermination of their allies, the ancient *ouloss* of Feka-Zechorr. The slight horses of the Cossacks were unable to support the weight of heavy Polish dragoons and a body of trained *cameleers* (that is, cuirassiers mounted on camels); hardy they were, but not strong, nor a match for their antagonists in weight; and their extraordinary efforts through the last few days to gain their present position had greatly diminished their powers for effecting an escape. Very few, in fact, *did* escape; and the bloody day of Ouchim became as memorable among the Cossacks as that which, about twenty days before, had signalized the complete annihilation of the Feka-Zechorr.[7]

The road was now open to the River Igritch, and as yet even far beyond it to the Torgau; but how long this state of things would continue was every day more doubtful. Certain intelligence was now received that a large Russian army, well appointed in every arm, was advancing upon the Torgau under the command of General Traubenberg. This officer was to be joined on his route by ten thousand Bashkirs, and pretty nearly the same amount of Kirghises—both hereditary enemies of the Kalmucks—both exasperated to a point of madness by the bloody trophies which Oubacha and Momotbacha had, in late years, won from such of their compatriots as served under the Sultan. The Czarina's yoke these wild nations bore with submissive patience, but not the hands by which it had been imposed; and accordingly, catching with eagerness at the present occasion offered to their vengeance, they sent an assurance to the Czarina of their perfect obedience to her commands, and at the same time a message significantly declaring in what spirit they meant to execute them—viz. "that they would not trouble her Majesty with prisoners."

Here then arose, as before with the Cossacks, a race for the Kalmucks with the regular armies of Russia, and concurrently with nations as fierce and semi-humanized as themselves, besides that they were stung into threefold activity by the furies of mortified pride and military abasement, under the eyes of the Turkish Sultan. The forces, and more especially the artillery, of Russia were far too overwhelming to permit the thought of a regular opposition in pitched battles, even with a less dilapidated state of their resources than they could reasonably expect at the period of their arrival on the Torgau. In their speed lay their only hope—in strength of foot, as before, and not in strength of arm. Onward, therefore, the Kalmucks pressed, marking the lines of their wide-extending march over the sad solitudes of the steppes by a never-ending chain of corpses. The old and the young, the sick man on his couch, the mother with her baby—all were left behind. Sights such as these, with the many

rueful aggravations incident to the helpless condition of
infancy—of disease and of female weakness abandoned
to the wolves amidst a howling wilderness—continued to 5
track their course through a space of full two thousand
miles; for so much at the least it was likely to prove,
including the circuits to which they were often compelled
by rivers or hostile tribes, from the point of starting on
the Wolga until they could reach their destined halting 10
ground on the east bank of the Torgau. For the first
seven weeks of this march their sufferings had been imbittered
by the excessive severity of the cold; and every
night—so long as wood was to be had for fires, either
from the lading of the camels, or from the desperate sacrifice 15
of their baggage wagons, or (as occasionally happened)
from the forests which skirted the banks of the many
rivers which crossed their path—no spectacle was more
frequent than that of a circle, composed of men, women,
and children, gathered by hundreds round a central fire, 20
all dead and stiff at the return of morning light. Myriads
were left behind from pure exhaustion, of whom none
had a chance, under the combined evils which beset
them, of surviving through the next twenty-four hours.
Frost, however, and snow at length ceased to persecute; 25
the vast extent of the march at length brought them into
more genial latitudes, and the unusual duration of the
march was gradually bringing them into more genial
seasons of the year. Two thousand miles had at least
been traversed; February, March, April, were gone; the 30
balmy month of May had opened; vernal sights and
sounds came from every side to comfort the heart-weary
travellers; and at last, in the latter end of May, crossing
the Torgau, they took up a position where they hoped to
find liberty to repose themselves for many weeks in comfort
as well as in security, and to draw such supplies from
the fertile neighborhood as might restore their shattered
forces to a condition for executing, with less of wreck
and ruin, the large remainder of the journey. 5

   Yes; it was true that two thousand miles of wandering
had been completed, but in a period of nearly five
months, and with the terrific sacrifice of at least two hundred
and fifty thousand souls, to say nothing of herds and

flocks past all reckoning. These had all perished: ox, 10
cow, horse, mule, ass, sheep, or goat, not one survived—only
the camels. These arid and adust creatures, looking
like the mummies of some antediluvian animals, without
the affections or sensibilities of flesh and blood—these
only still erected their speaking eyes to the eastern 15
heavens, and had to all appearance come out from this
long tempest of trial unscathed and hardly diminished.
The Khan, knowing how much he was individually
answerable for the misery which had been sustained,
must have wept tears even more bitter than those of 20
Xerxes when he threw his eyes over the myriads whom
he had assembled: for the tears of Xerxes were
unmingled with compunction. Whatever amends were in
his power, the Khan resolved to make, by sacrifices to
the general good of all personal regards; and, accordingly, 25
even at this point of their advance, he once more deliberately
brought under review the whole question of the
revolt. The question was formally debated before the
Council, whether, even at this point, they should untread
their steps, and, throwing themselves upon the Czarina's 30
mercy, return to their old allegiance. In that case,
Oubacha professed himself willing to become the scapegoat
for the general transgression. This, he argued, was
no fantastic scheme, but even easy of accomplishment;
for the unlimited and sacred power of the Khan, so well
known to the Empress, made it absolutely iniquitous to
attribute any separate responsibility to the people. Upon
the Khan rested the guilt—upon the Khan would
descend the imperial vengeance. This proposal was 5
applauded for its generosity, but was energetically opposed
by Zebek-Dorchi. Were they to lose the whole
journey of two thousand miles? Was their misery to
perish without fruit? True it was that they had yet
reached only the halfway house; but, in that respect, 10
the motives were evenly balanced for retreat or for
advance. Either way they would have pretty nearly
the same distance to traverse, but with this difference—that,
forwards, their route lay through lands comparatively
fertile; backwards, through a blasted wilderness, 15
rich only in memorials of their sorrow, and hideous to
Kalmuck eyes by the trophies of their calamity. Besides,

though the Empress might accept an excuse for the past, would she the less forbear to suspect for the future? The Czarina's *pardon* they might obtain, but could they 20 ever hope to recover her *confidence*? Doubtless there would now be a standing presumption against them, an immortal ground of jealousy; and a jealous government would be but another name for a harsh one. Finally, whatever motives there ever had been for the revolt 25 surely remained unimpaired by anything that had occurred. In reality the revolt was, after all, no revolt, but (strictly speaking) a return to their old allegiance; since, not above one hundred and fifty years ago (viz. in the year 1616), their ancestors had revolted from the 30 Emperor of China. They had now tried both governments; and for them China was the land of promise, and Russia the house of bondage.

Spite, however, of all that Zebek could say or do, the yearning of the people was strongly in behalf of the Khan's proposal; the pardon of their prince, they persuaded themselves, would be readily conceded by the Empress: and there is little doubt that they would at this time have thrown themselves gladly upon the imperial 5 mercy; when suddenly all was defeated by the arrival of two envoys from Traubenberg. This general had reached the fortress of Orsk, after a very painful march, on the 12th of April; thence he set forward toward Oriembourg, which he reached upon the 1st of June, having been 10 joined on his route at various times through the month of May by the Kirghises and a corps of ten thousand Bashkirs. From Oriembourg he sent forward his official offers to the Khan, which were harsh and peremptory, holding out no specific stipulations as to pardon or 15 impunity, an exacting unconditional submission as the preliminary price of any cessation from military operations. The personal character of Traubenberg, which was anything but energetic, and the condition of his army, disorganized in a great measure by the length and 20 severity of the march, made it probable that, with a little time for negotiation, a more conciliatory tone would have been assumed. But, unhappily for all parties, sinister events occurred in the meantime such as effectually put an end to every hope of the kind. 25

The two envoys sent forward by Traubenberg had
reported to this officer that a distance of only ten days'
march lay between his own headquarters and those of
the Khan. Upon this fact transpiring, the Kirghises, by
their prince Nourali, and the Bashkirs, entreated the 30
Russian general to advance without delay. Once having
placed his cannon in position, so as to command the
Kalmuck camp, the fate of the rebel Khan and his
people would be in his own hands, and they would
themselves form his advanced guard. Traubenberg, however
(*why* has not been certainly explained), refused to
march; grounding his refusal upon the condition of his
army and their absolute need of refreshment. Long
and fierce was the altercation; but at length, seeing no 5
chance of prevailing, and dreading above all other events
the escape of their detested enemy, the ferocious Bashkirs
went off in a body by forced marches. In six days
they reached the Torgau, crossed by swimming their
horses, and fell upon the Kalmucks, who were dispersed 10
for many a league in search of food or provender for
their camels. The first day's action was one vast succession
of independent skirmishes, diffused over a field
of thirty to forty miles in extent; one party often breaking
up into three or four, and again (according to the 15
accidents of ground) three or four blending into one;
flight and pursuit, rescue and total overthrow, going on
simultaneously, under all varieties of form, in all
quarters of the plain. The Bashkirs had found themselves obliged,
by the scattered state of the Kalmucks, to split up into 20
innumerable sections; and thus, for some hours, it had
been impossible for the most practised eye to collect the
general tendency of the day's fortune. Both the Khan
and Zebek-Dorchi were at one moment made prisoners,
and more than once in imminent danger of being cut 25
down; but at length Zebek succeeded in rallying a
strong column of infantry, which, with the support of the
camel corps on each flank, compelled the Bashkirs to
retreat. Clouds, however, of these wild cavalry continued
to arrive through the next two days and nights, followed 30
or accompanied by the Kirghises. These being viewed

as the advanced parties of Traubenberg's army, the
Kalmuck chieftains saw no hope of safety but in flight;
and in this way it happened that a retreat, which had so
recently been brought to a pause, was resumed at the
very moment when the unhappy fugitives were anticipating
a deep repose, without further molestation, the whole
summer through.

It seemed as though every variety of wretchedness 5
were predestined to the Kalmucks, and as if their sufferings
were incomplete unless they were rounded and
matured by all that the most dreadful agencies of summer's
heat could superadd to those of frost and winter.
To this sequel of their story we shall immediately revert, 10
after first noticing a little romantic episode which occurred
at this point between Oubacha and his unprincipled
cousin, Zebek-Dorchi.

There was, at the time of the Kalmuck flight from the
Wolga, a Russian gentleman of some rank at the court 15
of the Khan, whom, for political reasons, it was thought
necessary to carry along with them as a captive. For
some weeks his confinement had been very strict, and in
one or two instances cruel; but, as the increasing distance
was continually diminishing the chances of escape, 20
and perhaps, also, as the misery of the guards gradually
withdrew their attention from all minor interests to their
own personal sufferings, the vigilance of the custody
grew more and more relaxed; until at length, upon a
petition to the Khan, Mr. Weseloff was formally restored 25
to liberty; and it was understood that he might use his
liberty in whatever way he chose; even for returning
to Russia, if that should be his wish. Accordingly, he
was making active preparations for his journey to St.
Petersburg, when it occurred to Zebek-Dorchi that not 30
improbably, in some of the battles which were then anticipated
with Traubenberg, it might happen to them to
lose some prisoner of rank,—in which case the Russian
Weseloff would be a pledge in their hands for negotiating
an exchange. Upon this plea, to his own severe affliction,
the Russian was detained until the further pleasure
of the Khan. The Khan's name, indeed, was used
through the whole affair, but, as it seemed, with so little

concurrence on his part, that, when Wescloff in a private 5
audience humbly remonstrated upon the injustice done
him and the cruelty of thus sporting with his feelings by
setting him at liberty, and, as it were, tempting him into
dreams of home and restored happiness only for the purpose
of blighting them, the good-natured prince disclaimed 10
all participation in the affair, and went so far in
proving his sincerity as even to give him permission to
effect his escape; and, as a ready means of commencing
it without raising suspicion, the Khan mentioned to Mr.
Weseloff that he had just then received a message from 15
the Hetman of the Bashkirs, soliciting a private interview
on the banks of the Torgau at a spot pointed out. That
interview was arranged for the coming night; and Mr.
Weseloff might go in the Khan's *suite*, which on either
side was not to exceed three persons. Weseloff was a 20
prudent man, acquainted with the world, and he read
treachery in the very outline of this scheme, as stated by
the Khan—treachery against the Khan's person. He
mused a little, and then communicated so much of his
suspicions to the Khan as might put him on his guard; 25
but, upon further consideration, he begged leave to
decline the honor of accompanying the Khan. The fact
was that three Kalmucks, who had strong motives for
returning to their countrymen on the west bank of the
Wolga, guessing the intentions of Weseloff, had offered 30
to join him in his escape. These men the Khan would
probably find himself obliged to countenance in their
project, so that it became a point of honor with Weseloff
to conceal their intentions, and therefore to accomplish
the evasion from the camp (of which the first steps only
would be hazardous) without risking the notice of the
Khan.

The district in which they were now encamped
abounded through many hundred miles with wild horses 5
of a docile and beautiful breed. Each of the four fugitives
had caught from seven to ten of these spirited
creatures in the course of the last few days. This
raised no suspicion, for the rest of the Kalmucks had
been making the same sort of provision against the coming 10
toils of their remaining route to China. These horses

were secured by halters, and hidden about dusk in the
thickets which lined the margin of the river. To these
thickets, about ten at night, the four fugitives repaired.
They took a circuitous path, which drew them as little as 15
possible within danger of challenge from any of the outposts
or of the patrols which had been established on the
quarters where the Bashkirs lay; and in three-quarters of
an hour they reached the rendezvous. The moon had
now risen, the horses were unfastened; and they were 20
in the act of mounting, when the deep silence of the
woods was disturbed by a violent uproar and the clashing
of arms. Weseloff fancied that he heard the voice of
the Khan shouting for assistance. He remembered
the communication made by that prince in the morning; and, 25
requesting his companions to support him, he rode off in
the direction of the sound. A very short distance brought
him to an open glade in the wood, where he beheld four
men contending with a party of at least nine or ten.
Two of the four were dismounted at the very instant of 30
Weseloff's arrival. One of these he recognized almost
certainly as the Khan, who was fighting hand to hand,
but at great disadvantage, with two of the adverse horsemen.
Seeing that no time was to be lost, Weseloff fired
and brought down one of the two. His companions discharged
their carabines at the same moment; and then all
rushed simultaneously into the little open area. The
thundering sound of about thirty horses, all rushing at
once into a narrow space, gave the impression that a 5
whole troop of cavalry was coming down upon the assailants,
who accordingly wheeled about and fled with one
impulse. Weseloff advanced to the dismounted cavalier,
who, as he expected, proved to be the Khan. The man
whom Weseloff had shot was lying dead; and both were 10
shocked, though Weseloff at least was not surprised, on
stooping down and scrutinizing his features, to recognize
a well-known confidential servant of Zebek-Dorchi.
Nothing was said by either party. The Khan rode off,
escorted by Weseloff and his companions; and for some 15
time a dead silence prevailed. The situation of Weseloff
was delicate and critical. To leave the Khan at this point
was probably to cancel their recent services; for he might
be again crossed on his path, and again attacked, by the

very party from whom he had just been delivered. Yet, on 20
the other hand, to return to the camp was to endanger the
chances of accomplishing the escape. The Khan, also, was
apparently revolving all this in his mind; for at length he
broke silence and said: "I comprehend your situation;
and, under other circumstances, I might feel it my duty to 25
detain your companions, but it would ill become me to do
so after the important service you have just rendered me.
Let us turn a little to the left. There, where you see the
watch fire, is an outpost. Attend me so far. I am then
safe. You may turn and pursue your enterprise; for 30
the circumstances under which you will appear as my
escort are sufficient to shield you from all suspicion for
the present. I regret having no better means at my disposal
for testifying my gratitude. But tell me before we part—
was it accident only which led you to my rescue?
Or had you acquired any knowledge of the plot by which
I was decoyed into this snare?" Weseloff answered very
candidly that mere accident had brought him to the spot
at which he heard the uproar; but that, *having* heard it, 5
and connecting it with the Khan's communication of the
morning, he had then designedly gone after the sound in
a way which he certainly should not have done, at so
critical a moment, unless in the expectation of finding
the Khan assaulted by assassins. A few minutes after 10
they reached the outpost at which it became safe to
leave the Tartar chieftain; and immediately the four
fugitives commenced a flight which is, perhaps, without a
parallel in the annals of travelling. Each of them led
six or seven horses besides the one he rode; and by 15
shifting from one to the other (like the ancient Desultors
of the Roman circus), so as never to burden the same
horse for more than half an hour at a time, they continued
to advance at the rate of 200 miles in the twenty-four
hours for three days consecutively. After that time, 20
considering themselves beyond pursuit, they proceeded
less rapidly; though still with a velocity which staggered
the belief of Weseloff's friends in after years. He was,
however, a man of high principle, and always adhered
firmly to the details of his printed report. One of the 25
circumstances there stated is that they continued to pursue
the route by which the Kalmucks had fled, never for

an instant finding any difficulty in tracing it by the skeletons and other memorials of their calamities. In particular, he mentions vast heaps of money as part of the 30 valuable property which it had been necessary to sacrifice. These heaps were found lying still untouched in the deserts. From these Weseloff and his companions took as much as they could conveniently carry; and this it was, with the price of their beautiful horses, which they afterward sold at one of the Russian military settlements for about £15 apiece, which eventually enabled them to pursue their journey in Russia. This journey, as regarded Weseloff in particular, was closed by a tragical catastrophe. 5 He was at that time young and the only child of a doting mother. Her affliction under the violent abduction of her son had been excessive, and probably had undermined her constitution. Still she had supported it. Weseloff, giving way to the natural impulses of his filial 10 affection, had imprudently posted through Russia to his mother's house without warning of his approach. He rushed precipitately into her presence; and she, who had stood the shocks of sorrow, was found unequal to the shock of joy too sudden and too acute. She died upon 15 the spot.

We now revert to the final scenes of the Kalmuck flight. These it would be useless to pursue circumstantially through the whole two thousand miles of suffering which remained; for the character of that suffering was 20 even more monotonous than on the former half of the flight, but also more severe. Its main elements were excessive heat, with the accompaniments of famine and thirst, but aggravated at every step by the murderous attacks of their cruel enemies, the Bashkirs and the 25 Kirghises.

These people, "more fell than anguish, hunger, or the sea," stuck to the unhappy Kalmucks like a swarm of enraged hornets. And very often, while *they* were attacking them in the rear, their advanced parties and 30 flanks were attacked with almost equal fury by the people of the country which they were traversing; and with good

reason, since the law of self-preservation had now obliged
the fugitive Tartars to plunder provisions and to forage
wherever they passed. In this respect their condition
was a constant oscillation of wretchedness; for sometimes,
pressed by grinding famine, they took a circuit of
perhaps a hundred miles, in order to strike into a land 5
rich in the comforts of life; but in such a land they were
sure to find a crowded population, of which every arm
was raised in unrelenting hostility, with all the advantages
of local knowledge, and with constant preoccupation of
all the defensible positions, mountain passes, or bridges. 10
Sometimes, again, wearied out with this mode of suffering,
they took a circuit of perhaps a hundred miles, in
order to strike into a land with few or no inhabitants.
But in such a land they were sure to meet absolute
starvation. Then, again, whether with or without this 15
plague of starvation, whether with or without this plague
of hostility in front, whatever might be the "fierce varieties"
of their misery in this respect, no rest ever came
to their unhappy rear; *post equitem sedet atra cura*: it
was a torment like the undying worm of conscience. 20
And, upon the whole, it presented a spectacle altogether
unprecedented in the history of mankind. Private and
personal malignity is not unfrequently immortal; but rare
indeed is it to find the same pertinacity of malice in
a nation. And what imbittered the interest was that the 25
malice was reciprocal. Thus far the parties met upon
equal terms; but that equality only sharpened the sense
of their dire inequality as to other circumstances. The
Bashkirs were ready to fight "from morn till dewy eve."
The Kalmucks, on the contrary, were always obliged to 30
run. Was it *from* their enemies as creatures whom they
feared? No; but *towards* their friends—towards that
final haven of China—as what was hourly implored by
the prayers of their wives and the tears of their children.
But, though they fled unwillingly, too often they fled in
vain—being unwillingly recalled. There lay the torment.
Every day the Bashkirs fell upon them; every
day the same unprofitable battle was renewed; as a
matter of course, the Kalmucks recalled part of their 5
advanced guard to fight them; every day the battle raged
for hours, and uniformly with the same result. For, no

sooner did the Bashkirs find themselves too heavily
pressed, and that the Kalmuck march had been retarded
by some hours, than they retired into the boundless 10
deserts, where all pursuit was hopeless. But if the Kalmucks
resolved to press forwards, regardless of their enemies—in
that case their attacks became so fierce and
overwhelming that the general safety seemed likely to be
brought into question; nor could any effectual remedy 15
be applied to the case, even for each separate day, except
by a most embarrassing halt and by countermarches
that, to men in their circumstances, were almost worse
than death. It will not be surprising that the irritation
of such a systematic persecution, superadded to a previous, 20
and hereditary hatred, and accompanied by the
stinging consciousness of utter impotence as regarded all
effectual vengeance, should gradually have inflamed the
Kalmuck animosity into the wildest expression of downright
madness and frenzy. Indeed, long before the 25
frontiers of China were approached, the hostility of both
sides had assumed the appearance much more of a
warfare amongst wild beasts than amongst creatures
acknowledging the restraints of reason or the claims of a
common nature. The spectacle became too atrocious; it 30
was that of a host of lunatics pursued by a host of fiends.

On a fine morning in early autumn of the year 1771,
Kien Long, the Emperor of China, was pursuing his
amusements in a wild frontier district lying on the outside
of the Great Wall. For many hundred square
leagues the country was desolate of inhabitants, but rich
in woods of ancient growth, and overrun with game of
every description. In a central spot of this solitary 5
region the Emperor had built a gorgeous hunting lodge,
to which he resorted annually for recreation and relief
from the cares of government. Led onwards in pursuit of
game, he had rambled to a distance of 200 miles or
more from his lodge, followed at a little distance by a 10
sufficient military escort, and every night pitching his
tent in a different situation, until at length he had arrived
on the very margin of the vast central deserts of Asia.[8]
Here he was standing by accident, at an opening of his

pavilion, enjoying the morning sunshine, when suddenly 15
to the westward there arose a vast, cloudy vapor, which
by degrees expanded, mounted, and seemed to be slowly
diffusing itself over the whole face of the heavens. By
and by this vast sheet of mist began to thicken toward
the horizon and to roll forward in billowy volumes. The 20
Emperor's suite assembled from all quarters; the silver
trumpets were sounded in the rear; and from all the
glades and forest avenues began to trot forwards towards
the pavilion the yagers—half cavalry, half huntsmen—who
composed the imperial escort. Conjecture was on 25
the stretch to divine the cause of this phenomenon; and
the interest continually increased in proportion as simple
curiosity gradually deepened into the anxiety of uncertain
danger. At first it had been imagined that some vast
troops of deer or other wild animals of the chase had
been disturbed in their forest haunts by the Emperor's
movements, or possibly by wild beasts prowling for prey,
and might be fetching a compass by way of re-entering
the forest grounds at some remoter points, secure from 5
molestation. But this conjecture was dissipated by the
slow increase of the cloud and the steadiness of its
motion. In the course of two hours the vast phenomenon
had advanced to a point which was judged to be
within five miles of the spectators, though all calculations 10
of distance were difficult, and often fallacious, when
applied to the endless expanses of the Tartar deserts.
Through the next hour, during which the gentle morning
breeze had a little freshened, the dusty vapor had developed
itself far and wide into the appearance of huge 15
aërial draperies, hanging in mighty volumes from the sky
to the earth; and at particular points, where the eddies
of the breeze acted upon the pendulous skirts of these
aërial curtains, rents were perceived, sometimes taking the
form of regular arches, portals, and windows, through 20
which began dimly to gleam the heads of camels "indorsed"[9]
with human beings, and at intervals the moving
of men and horses in tumultuous array, and then through
other openings, or vistas, at far-distant points, the flashing
of polished arms. But sometimes, as the wind slackened 25
or died away, all those openings, of whatever form,
in the cloudy pall, would slowly close, and for a time the

whole pageant was shut up from view; although the
growing din, the clamors, the shrieks, and groans ascending
from infuriated myriads, reported, in a language not 30
to be misunderstood, what was going on behind the
cloudy screen.

   It was, in fact, the Kalmuck host, now in the last extremities of
their exhaustion, and very fast approaching
to that final stage of privation and killing misery beyond
which few or none could have lived, but also, happily for
themselves, fast approaching (in a literal sense) that final 5
stage of their long pilgrimage at which they would meet
hospitality on a scale of royal magnificence and full protection
from their enemies. These enemies, however, as
yet, still were hanging on their rear as fiercely as ever,
though this day was destined to be the last of their hideous 10
persecution. The Khan had, in fact, sent forward
couriers with all the requisite statements and petitions,
addressed to the Emperor of China. These had been
duly received, and preparations made in consequence to
welcome the Kalmucks with the most paternal benevolence. 15
But as these couriers had been dispatched from
the Torgau at the moment of arrival thither, and before
the advance of Traubenberg had made it necessary
for the Khan to order a hasty renewal of the flight, the
Emperor had not looked for their arrival on his frontiers 20
until full three months after the present time. The Khan
had, indeed, expressly notified his intention to pass the
summer heats on the banks of the Torgau, and to recommence
his retreat about the beginning of September. The
subsequent change of plan being unknown to Kien Long, 25
left him for some time in doubt as to the true interpretation
to be put upon this mighty apparition in the desert:
but at length the savage clamors of hostile fury and
clangor of weapons unveiled to the Emperor the true
nature of those unexpected calamities which had so prematurely
30
precipitated the Kalmuck measure.

   Apprehending the real state of affairs, the Emperor
instantly perceived that the first act of his fatherly care
for these erring children (as he esteemed them), now
returning to their ancient obedience, must be—to deliver

them from their pursuers. And this was less difficult
than might have been supposed. Not many miles in the
rear was a body of well-appointed cavalry, with a strong
detachment of artillery, who always attended the Emperor's 5
motions. These were hastily summoned. Meantime
it occurred to the train of courtiers that some danger
might arise to the Emperor's person from the proximity
of a lawless enemy, and accordingly he was induced to
retire a little to the rear. It soon appeared, however, to 10
those who watched the vapory shroud in the desert, that
its motion was not such as would argue the direction of
the march to be exactly upon the pavilion, but rather in
a diagonal line, making an angle of full 45 degrees with
that line in which the imperial *cortége* had been standing, 15
and therefore with a distance continually increasing.
Those who knew the country judged that the Kalmucks
were making for a large fresh-water lake about seven or
eight miles distant. They were right; and to that point
the imperial cavalry was ordered up; and it was precisely 20
in that spot, and about three hours after, and at noonday
on the 8th of September, that the great Exodus of the
Kalmuck Tartars was brought to a final close, and with a
scene of such memorable and hellish fury as formed an
appropriate winding up to an expedition in all its parts 25
and details so awfully disastrous. The Emperor was not
personally present, or at least he saw whatever he *did* see
from too great a distance to discriminate its individual
features; but he records in his written memorial the
report made to him of this scene by some of his own 30
officers.

　　The Lake of Tengis, near the frightful Desert of Kobi,
lay in a hollow amongst hills of a moderate height, ranging
generally from two to three thousand feet high. About
eleven o'clock in the forenoon, the Chinese cavalry
reached the summit of a road which led through a cradle-like
dip in the mountains right down upon the margin of
the lake. From this pass, elevated about two thousand
feet above the level of the water, they continued to 5
descend, by a very winding and difficult road, for an hour
and a half; and during the whole of this descent they were
compelled to be inactive spectators of the fiendish spectacle

below. The Kalmucks, reduced by this time from about six hundred thousand souls to two hundred and 10 sixty thousand, and after enduring for two months and a half the miseries we have previously described—outrageous heat, famine, and the destroying scimiter of the Kirghises and the Bashkirs—had for the last ten days been traversing a hideous desert, where no vestiges were 15 seen of vegetation, and no drop of water could be found. Camels and men were already so overladen that it was a mere impossibility that they should carry a tolerable sufficiency for the passage of this frightful wilderness. On the eighth day the wretched daily allowance, which had 20 been continually diminishing, failed entirely; and thus, for two days of insupportable fatigue, the horrors of thirst had been carried to the fiercest extremity. Upon this last morning, at the sight of the hills and the forest scenery, which announced to those who acted as guides 25 the neighborhood of the Lake of Tengis, all the people rushed along with maddening eagerness to the anticipated solace. The day grew hotter and hotter, the people more and more exhausted; and gradually, in the general rush forward to the lake, all discipline and command were lost—all 30 attempts to preserve a rear guard were neglected—the wild Bashkirs rode on amongst the encumbered people and slaughtered them by wholesale, and almost without resistance. Screams and tumultuous shouts proclaimed the progress of the massacre; but none heeded—none halted; all alike, pauper or noble, continued to rush on with maniacal haste to the waters—all with faces blackened by the heat preying upon the liver and with tongue drooping from the mouth. The cruel Bashkir was 5 affected by the same misery, and manifested the same symptoms of his misery, as the wretched Kalmuck; the murderer was oftentimes in the same frantic misery as his murdered victim—many, indeed (an ordinary effect of thirst), in both nations had become lunatic, and in this 10 state, whilst mere multitude and condensation of bodies alone opposed any check to the destroying scimiter and the trampling hoof, the lake was reached; and to that the whole vast body of enemies rushed, and together continued to rush, forgetful of all things at that moment 15 but of one almighty instinct. This absorption of the thoughts in one maddening appetite lasted for a single half hour; but in the next arose the final scene of parting vengeance. Far and wide the waters of the solitary lake were instantly dyed red with blood and gore: here rode a 20 party of savage Bashkirs, hewing off heads as fast as the swaths fall before the mower's scythe; there stood unarmed Kalmucks in a death grapple with their detested foes, both up to the middle in water, and oftentimes both sinking together below the surface, from weakness or from 25 struggles, and perishing in each other's arms. Did the Bashkirs at any point collect into a cluster for the sake of giving impetus to the assault? Thither were the camels driven in fiercely by those who rode them, generally women or boys; and even these quiet creatures were 30 forced into a share in this carnival of murder by trampling down as many as they could strike prostrate with the lash of their fore-legs. Every moment the water grew more polluted; and yet every moment fresh myriads came up to the lake and rushed in, not able to resist their frantic thirst, and swallowing large draughts of water, visibly contaminated with the blood of their slaughtered compatriots. Wheresoever the lake was shallow enough to allow of men raising their heads above the water, there, 5 for scores of acres, were to be seen all forms of ghastly fear, of agonizing struggle, of spasm, of death, and the fear of death—revenge, and the lunacy of revenge—until the neutral spectators, of whom there were not a few, now descending the eastern side of the lake, at length 10 averted their eyes in horror. This horror, which seemed incapable of further addition, was, however, increased by an unexpected incident. The Bashkirs, beginning to perceive here and there the approach of the Chinese cavalry, felt it prudent—wheresoever they were sufficiently 15 at leisure from the passions of the murderous scene—to gather into bodies. This was noticed by the governor of a small Chinese fort built upon an eminence above the lake; and immediately he threw in a broadside, which spread havoc among the Bashkir tribe. As often 20 as the Bashkirs collected into *globes* and *turms* as their only means of meeting the long line of descending Chinese cavalry, so often did the Chinese governor of the fort pour in his exterminating broadside; until at length

the lake, at its lower end, became one vast seething 25
caldron of human bloodshed and carnage. The Chinese
cavalry had reached the foot of the hills; the Bashkirs,
attentive to *their* movements, had formed; skirmishes had
been fought; and, with a quick sense that the contest was
henceforward rapidly becoming hopeless, the Bashkirs 30
and Kirghises began to retire. The pursuit was not as
vigorous as the Kalmuck hatred would have desired.
But, at the same time, the very gloomiest hatred could
not but find, in their own dreadful experience of the
Asiatic deserts, and in the certainty that these wretched
Bashkirs had to repeat that same experience a second
time, for thousands of miles, as the price exacted by a
retributary Providence for their vindictive cruelty—not
the very gloomiest of the Kalmucks, or the least reflecting, 5
but found in all this a retaliatory chastisement more
complete and absolute than any which their swords and
lances could have obtained or human vengeance could
have devised.

––––––––––––––––––––

Here ends the tale of the Kalmuck wanderings in the 10
Desert; for any subsequent marches which awaited them
were neither long nor painful. Every possible alleviation
and refreshment for their exhausted bodies had been
already provided by Kien Long with the most princely
munificence; and lands of great fertility were immediately 15
assigned to them in ample extent along the River Ily, not
very far from the point at which they had first emerged
from the wilderness of Kobi. But the beneficent attention
of the Chinese Emperor may be best stated in his own
words, as translated into French by one of the Jesuit 20
missionaries: "La nation des Torgotes (*savoir les Kalmuques*)
arriva à Ily, toute delabrée, n'ayant ni de quoi vivre, ni de quoi
se vêtir. Je l'avais prévu; et j'avais
ordonné de faire en tout genre les provisions nécessaires
pour pouvoir les secourir promptement: c'est ce qui a été 25
exécuté. On a fait la division des terres: et on a assigné
à chaque famille une portion suffisante pour pouvoir servir
à son entretien, soit en la cultivant, soit en y nourrissant
des bestiaux. On a donné à chaque particulier des étoffes
pour l'habiller, des grains pour se nourrir pendant l'éspace 30

d'une année, des ustensiles pour le ménage et d'autres choses nécessaires: et outre cela plusieurs onces d'argent, pour se pourvoir de ce qu'on aurait pu oublier. On a designé des lieux particuliers, fertiles en pâturages; et on leur a donné des boeufs, moutons, etc., pour qu'ils pussent dans la suite travailler par eux-mêmes à leur entretien et à leur bien-être."

These are the words of the Emperor himself, speaking 5 in his own person of his own paternal cares; but another Chinese, treating the same subject, records the munificence of this prince in terms which proclaim still more forcibly the disinterested generosity which prompted, and the delicate considerateness which conducted, this extensive 10 bounty. He has been speaking of the Kalmucks, and he goes on thus:—"Lorsqu'ils arrivèrent sur nos frontières (au nombre de plusieurs centaines de mille, quoique la fatigue extrême, la faim, la soif, et toutes les autres incommodités inséparables d'une très-longue et 15 très-pénible route en eussent fait périr presque autant), ils étaient réduits à la dernière misère; ils manquaient de tout. Il" (viz. l'empereur, Kien Long) "leur fit préparer des logemens conformes à leur manière de vivre; il leur fit distribuer des alimens et des habits; il leur fit 20 donner des boeufs, des moutons, et des ustensiles, pour les mettre en état de former des troupeaux et de cultiver la terre, et tout cela à ses propres frais, qui se sont montés à des sommes immenses, sans compter l'argent qu'il a donné à chaque chef-de-famille, pour pouvoir à la 25 subsistance de sa femme et de ses enfans."

Thus, after their memorable year of misery, the Kalmucks were replaced in territorial possessions, and in comfort equal, perhaps, or even superior, to that which they had enjoyed in Russia, and with superior political 30 advantages. But, if equal or superior, their condition was no longer the same; if not in degree, their social prosperity had altered in quality; for, instead of being a purely pastoral and vagrant people, they were now in circumstances which obliged them to become essentially dependent upon agriculture; and thus far raised in social rank that, by the natural course of their habits and the necessities of life, they were effectually reclaimed from

roving and from the savage customs connected with a half 5
nomadic life. They gained also in political privileges,
chiefly through the immunity from military service which
their new relations enabled them to obtain. These were
circumstances of advantage and gain. But one great
disadvantage there was, amply to overbalance all other 10
possible gain: the chances were lost, or were removed to
an incalculable distance, for their conversion to Christianity,
without which in these times there is no absolute
advance possible on the path of true civilization.

One word remains to be said upon the *personal* interests 15
concerned in this great drama. The catastrophe in this
respect was remarkable and complete. Oubacha, with all
his goodness and incapacity of suspecting, had, since the
mysterious affair on the banks of the Torgau, felt his
mind alienated from his cousin; he revolted from the man 20
that would have murdered him; and he had displayed his
caution so visibly as to provoke a reaction in the bearing
of Zebek-Dorchi and a displeasure which all his dissimulation
could not hide. This had produced a feud, which,
by keeping them aloof, had probably saved the life of 25
Oubacha; for the friendship of Zebek-Dorchi was more
fatal than his open enmity. After the settlement on the
Ily this feud continued to advance, until it came under
the notice of the Emperor, on occasion of a visit which
all the Tartar chieftains made to his Majesty at his hunting 30
lodge in 1772. The Emperor informed himself accurately
of all the particulars connected with the transaction—of
all the rights and claims put forward—and of the
way in which they would severally affect the interests of
the Kalmuck people. The consequence was that he
adopted the cause of Oubacha, and repressed the pretensions
of Zebek-Dorchi, who, on his part, so deeply
resented this discountenance to his ambitious projects
that, in conjunction with other chiefs, he had the presumption 5
even to weave nets of treason against the Emperor
himself. Plots were laid, were detected, were baffled;
counter-plots were constructed upon the same basis,
and with the benefit of the opportunities thus offered.
Finally, Zebek-Dorchi was invited to the imperial lodge, 10
together with all his accomplices; and, under the skilful

management of the Chinese nobles in the Emperor's establishment, the murderous artifices of these Tartar chieftains were made to recoil upon themselves, and the whole of them perished by assassination at a great imperial 15 banquet. For the Chinese morality is exactly of that kind which approves in everything the *lex talionis*:

"... Lex nec justior ulla est [as *they* think]
Quam necis artifices arte perire sua."

So perished Zebek-Dorchi, the author and originator of 20 the great Tartar Exodus. Oubacha, meantime, and his people were gradually recovering from the effects of their misery, and repairing their losses. Peace and prosperity, under the gentle rule of a fatherly lord paramount, redawned upon the tribes: their household *lares*, after so 25 harsh a translation to distant climates, found again a happy reinstatement in what had, in fact, been their primitive abodes: they found themselves settled in quiet sylvan scenes, rich in all the luxuries of life, and endowed with the perfect loveliness of Arcadian beauty. But from 30 the hills of this favored land, and even from the level grounds as they approach its western border, they still look out upon that fearful wilderness which once beheld a nation in agony—the utter extirpation of nearly half a million from amongst its numbers, and for the remainder a storm of misery so fierce that in the end (as happened also at Athens during the Peloponnesian war from a different 5 form of misery) very many lost their memory; all records of their past life were wiped out as with a sponge —utterly erased and cancelled: and many others lost their reason; some in a gentle form of pensive melancholy, some in a more restless form of feverish delirium 10 and nervous agitation, and others in the fixed forms of tempestuous mania, raving frenzy, or moping idiocy. Two great commemorative monuments arose in after years to mark the depth and permanence of the awe— the sacred and reverential grief, with which all persons looked back upon the dread calamities attached to the 15 year of the tiger—all who had either personally shared in those calamities and had themselves drunk from that cup of sorrow, or who had effectually been made witnesses to their results and associated with their relief: two great

monuments; one embodied in the religious solemnity, 20
enjoined by the Dalai-Lama, called in the Tartar language
a *Romanang*—that is, a national commemoration, with
music the most rich and solemn, of all the souls who
departed to the rest of Paradise from the afflictions of the
Desert (this took place about six years after the arrival 25
in China); secondly, another, more durable, and more
commensurate to the scale of the calamity and to the
grandeur of this national Exodus, in the mighty columns
of granite and brass erected by the Emperor, Kien Long,
near the banks of the Ily. These columns stand upon 30
the very margin of the steppes, and they bear a short but
emphatic inscription[10] to the following effect:—

By the Will of God,
Here, upon the Brink of these Deserts,
Which from this point begin and stretch away,
Pathless, treeless, waterless,
For thousands of miles, and along the margins of
many mighty 5
Nations,
Rested from their labors and from great
afflictions
Under the shadow of the Chinese Wall,
And by the favor of KIEN LONG, God's Lieutenant
upon Earth,
The ancient Children of the Wilderness—the
Torgote Tartars— 10
Flying before the wrath of the Grecian Czar,
Wandering Sheep who had strayed away from the
Celestial Empire
in the year 1616,
But are now mercifully gathered again, after
infinite sorrow,
Into the fold of their forgiving Shepherd. 15
Hallowed be the spot
and
Hallowed be the day—September 8, 1771!
Amen.